James Hadley Chase and The Murder Room

››› This title is part of The Murder Room, our series dedicated to making available out-of-print or hard-to-find titles by classic crime writers.

Crime fiction has always held up a mirror to society. The Victorians were fascinated by sensational murder and the emerging science of detection; now we are obsessed with the forensic detail of violent death. And no other genre has so captivated and enthralled readers.

Vast troves of classic crime writing have for a long time been unavailable to all but the most dedicated frequenters of second-hand bookshops. The advent of digital publishing means that we are now able to bring you the backlists of a huge range of titles by classic and contemporary crime writers, some of which have been out of print for decades.

From the genteel amateur private eyes of the Golden Age and the femmes fatales of pulp fiction, to the morally ambiguous hard-boiled detectives of mid twentieth-century America and their descendants who walk our twenty-first century streets, The Murder Room has it all. ›››

The Murder Room
Where Criminal Minds Meet

themurderroom.com

T0352440

James Hadley Chase (1906–1985)

Born René Brabazon Raymond in London, the son of a British colonel in the Indian Army, James Hadley Chase was educated at King's School in Rochester, Kent, and left home at the age of 18. He initially worked in book sales until, inspired by the rise of gangster culture during the Depression and by reading James M. Cain's *The Postman Always Rings Twice*, he wrote his first novel, *No Orchids for Miss Blandish.* Despite the American setting of many of his novels, Chase (like Peter Cheyney, another hugely successful British noir writer) never lived there, writing with the aid of maps and a slang dictionary. He had phenomenal success with the novel, which continued unabated throughout his entire career, spanning 45 years and nearly 90 novels. His work was published in dozens of languages and over thirty titles were adapted for film. He served in the RAF during World War II, where he also edited the RAF Journal. In 1956 he moved to France with his wife and son; they later moved to Switzerland, where Chase lived until his death in 1985.

By James Hadley Chase
(published in The Murder Room)

No Orchids for Miss Blandish
Eve
More Deadly Than the Male
Mission to Venice
Mission to Siena
Not Safe to Be Free
Shock Treatment
Come Easy – Go Easy
What's Better Than Money?
Just Another Sucker
I Would Rather Stay Poor
A Coffin from Hong Kong
Tell it to the Birds
One Bright Summer Morning
The Soft Centre
You Have Yourself a Deal
Have This One on Me
Well Now, My Pretty
Believed Violent
An Ear to the Ground
The Whiff of Money
The Vulture Is a Patient Bird
Like a Hole in the Head
An Ace Up My Sleeve
Want to Stay Alive?
Just a Matter of Time
You're Dead Without Money
Have a Change of Scene
Knock, Knock! Who's There?
Goldfish Have No Hiding Place
So What Happens to Me?
The Joker in the Pack
Believe This, You'll Believe Anything
Do Me a Favour – Drop Dead
I Hold the Four Aces
My Laugh Comes Last
Consider Yourself Dead
You Must Be Kidding
A Can of Worms
Try This One for Size
You Can Say That Again
Hand Me a Fig-Leaf
Have a Nice Night
We'll Share a Double Funeral
Not My Thing
Hit Them Where It Hurts

Believed Violent

James Hadley Chase

An Orion book

This edition published by
The Orion Publishing Group Ltd
Orion House
5 Upper St Martin's Lane
London WC2H 9EA

An Hachette UK company
A CIP catalogue record for this book is available from the British Library

ISBN 978 1 4719 0360 1

www.orionbooks.co.uk

CURTAIN RAISER

'DON'T MOVE,' she said breathlessly, her fingers moving down the length of his naked back. 'Stay still . . . don't move.'

So he waited, pressed down on her, knowing from experience to let her have her way, knowing that when she was ready she would suddenly become an eel-like thing, and they would be transported into an explosive fusion that would create yet another memorable moment of lust.

Their clothes, discarded in the frenzy of desire, lay by the bed in disorderly heaps.

As she suddenly arched her body, her breathing becoming convulsive, the bedroom door opened silently. Neither of them became aware that a third person had joined them.

The tall man stood motionless, watching them. When she cried out—a cry he had only heard once during their miserable marriage—he closed the door and moved back into the untidy sitting-room.

The room with his and her things scattered around, with dust on the occasional tables and on the face of the television set, with the ashtrays still unemptied, with all his papers, his books and the unopened mail became four dimensional. He found he was no longer able to focus. Everything in the room he looked at became blurred and distorted.

As he heard her cry out again, he pressed the cold palms of his hands against his temples. Then through the bedroom door, he heard her moan, a sound that could have come from the throat of an animal.

The fragile thread that had been holding his reason together snapped. This thread had been under threat for some months. Sooner or later, it was certain to break. It was unfortunate for the man in the bedroom that it snapped at this moment.

The tall man suddenly felt lighter. Everything in the room came abruptly into focus. He paid no further attention to the sounds coming from the bedroom. He walked silently out of the sitting-room and across the lobby and into the kitchen with all the gadgets that she had insisted he should buy as status symbols and which she never used. He took from one of the drawers a barbecue knife she had given him as a Christmas present. Its four inch blade glittered in the beam of the sunlight coming through the kitchen window. The wooden handle, studded with brass-headed nails, fitted comfortably into his cold grasp.

He returned to the sitting-room and waited, standing by the window where he could see the low wooden huts of the Experimental Station where he had worked with ceaseless application for the past three years. He waited for some twenty minutes and from time to time, he tested the edge of the knife which was razor sharp. Then he heard his wife say, 'I must have a drink. Go on, darling . . . for God's sake, get off me! I'm dying for a drink!'

He walked silently to the bedroom door, holding the knife by his side. He heard the sound of movement. He heard the one man he had regarded with trust, say, 'Who wants a drink, baby? I know what I want.'

'Get me a drink!' There was that snap in her voice that always dominated any man. 'We have all the time in the world. He won't be back until tomorrow.'

'Okay. Maybe I could use a drink myself, but you stay right where you are . . . understand?'

He heard her laugh.

'I'm not going to run away.'

The bed creaked—the bed he hadn't shared with her now for a long time. He listened to the sound of naked feet padding over the parquet floor. The door swung open.

The two men confronted each other. The tall man drove the blade of the knife forward and down, then ripped up.

The man he thought he could trust fell against him, sending him staggering back. This gave the woman, lying naked on the bed, time to save her life. She had instant reflexes. She was off the bed and had slammed and locked the door before the tall man could reach her.

But she knew she was within only a few heartbeats away from a horrible death. She snatched up the telephone receiver and screamed to the startled operator, 'Come quickly . . . I'm being murdered!'

Then as the bedroom door shuddered under the maniacal attack, she fled into the bathroom, slammed and bolted the door. She began to scream through the high window, too small for an escape.

CHAPTER ONE

Herman Radnitz crossed the entrance hall of the Bristol Hotel Kempinski and handed the Hall Porter his room key.

'Good evening, sir.' The Hall Porter gave a little bow, reserved only for the most important clients staying at the best hotel in West Berlin. 'Your car is waiting.'

Radnitz nodded. He was a square shaped, fat man with hooded eyes and a thick, hooked nose. Internationally known as one of the richest men in the world with financial machinations spread like the tentacles of an octopus over the whole globe, Radnitz wielded enormous power over Foreign Embassies, the Gnomes of Zurich and the New York and London Stock markets. He was a deadly spider, sitting in the middle of his financial web, snapping at every unwary fly that could add to his vast wealth.

He was wearing a black Broadtail cap and a black cloth overcoat, lined with dark wild mink. The diamond of his stick pin, in his black silk cravat, was of the quality a Rajah would have envied. He exuded power, money and luxury living. It was only when one looked directly into the hooded slate grey eyes that the cold ruthlessness of his nature became startlingly apparent.

He made his way to the double glass doors. The doorman, waiting, held open the doors. He lifted his peak cap and bowed. Radnitz ignored him. He walked down the steps into the bracing cold air where Ko-Yu, his Japanese servant and chauffeur, stood waiting by the black and silver Rolls-Royce.

'I have an appointment at the Brandenburg Gate at 11 o'clock. You will have to allow forty minutes to pass the frontier,' Radnitz said. 'I will leave the timing to you.'

He got into the car and Ko-Yu shut the car door. He slid into the driver's seat. The car moved off.

Radnitz selected a cigar from the cedar-wood box, built into the elaborate cocktail cabinet that faced him. The Rolls had been built to his specifications. It lacked nothing: the cocktail cabinet, a short wave receiving and sending set, a Sony television set, a telephone, a tiny refrigerator and an electrically heated box where a hot meal could be kept. He lit the cigar, then switching on a pilot light, he took papers from his brief-case and began to study them.

Ten minutes later, the car slowed. They had reached the West

Berlin terminus. Facing them was a big sign in English, German and Russian that read:

You are now leaving the American sector of Berlin.

A guard waved them through with a cheerful grin. Now, driving at a snail's pace, the Rolls approached the big red and white steel pole, set across the road in concrete pillars that blocked the way into East Berlin. The car stopped. A fur capped guard, pistol at his hip, stared into the car. Radnitz handed him his passport through the open window. His fat face was expressionless. He wanted no trouble. His business beyond the barrier was far too important to risk upsetting some touchy guard. The passport was handed back, the barrier raised and the Rolls moved into a no-man's land. Ahead, was a cunningly constructed maze of concrete blocks so formed that no car could get up enough speed to crash through the barrier. To the right was a row of wooden huts. A few cars were parked near the huts. Ko-Yu, who had been briefed by the Hall Porter, drew up, got out and opened the door of the car. He followed Radnitz into the first of the huts. Their passports were checked, then they were given forms to complete. As Ko-Yu wrote poor English, Radnitz completed both forms: name, nationality, birthplace and how much money each man was carrying. Ko-Yu had no money. Radnitz had DM.1000. They went to another desk and handed over their completed forms. Their passports were again examined. Both men were asked to show the contents of their wallets. Ko-Yu had no wallet and giggled uneasily. His fat face still expressionless, Radnitz revealed the contents of his gold-edged, seal-skin wallet. He was given four small red tickets and waved to another hut. Here he exchanged two West Berlin DM.5 bills (one for himself and one for Ko-Yu) for two East Berlin DM.5 bills, a compulsory exchange that gave the Communists a steady trickle of hard currency.

Leaving the hut, they found a guard walking suspiciously around the Rolls. Radnitz had been warned the search would be thorough, and it was. While he stood back, Ko-Yu and the guard removed the seats from the Rolls. The engine and the boot were examined. Working with a powerful flashlight, the guard took his time. Finally, he produced a three foot wide mirror, mounted on wheels which he pushed under the car, using his flashlight to reflect the underneath of the car. Then satisfied there was no one concealed there, he waved them on.

Radnitz got back into the car and Ko-Yu drove him through

the maze of concrete until they reached yet another barrier. Again their passports were examined and Radnitz handed over the red tickets, then the barrier was raised and they drove into East Berlin.

'Careful people,' Ko-Yu remarked and giggled.

Radnitz wasn't in the mood for such a remark. He glanced at his watch. They had three minutes before his appointment. He had no need to tell Ko-Yu the way. Ko-Yu always knew the way, no matter in what country he was driving. He was the best and the most intelligent chauffeur Radnitz had found. He was also the best cook, the best valet and houseboy, and Radnitz paid him accordingly.

The Rolls moved along Friedrichstrasse, turned left at Unter Den Linden, and in a few seconds came in sight of the Brandenburg Gate, floodlit and impressive in the big, deserted square where it stood.

'Stop here,' Radnitz said, then pressed a button that raised the glass partition between himself and his chauffeur.

As the car pulled up, a stocky man came out of the shadows. Even in the poor light, it could be seen that he was shabby. His trousers were baggy, his hat shapeless, his dark overcoat hung anyhow. He came up to the car as Radnitz, who recognized him, opened the car door. The man whose name was Igor Douzenski got into the car. He settled himself beside Radnitz who picked up the hand microphone and told Ko-Yu to drive around.

'Not quickly . . . just keep driving,' and he turned off the microphone.

'Well, my friend,' he said to Douzenski, 'I hope we can now finalize this affair. Your country, of course, is not the only one interested. Enough time has already been wasted.'

Douzenski folded his grimy hands in his lap. The heating in the car after the long cold wait was relaxing. The smell of the expensive cigar, blending with Radnitz's after-shave lotion, made him aware of his own bitter poverty. If this Capitalist, whom he and his Government suspected to be crooked, hoped to intimidate him, he was in for a surprise.

'We can't be overheard?' he asked, speaking in German.

'No.'

'Your chauffeur is reliable?'

'Yes.' Radnitz's cryptic answers showed his boredom. There was a pause, then Douzenski said, 'I have consulted my people. They think it is most unlikely that what you offer could become a reality.'

Radnitz drew on his cigar.

'That I can appreciate. I too was doubtful, but I am now satisfied it can be arranged. Briefly. I can give your Government Formula ZCX.'

'That I can believe,' Douzenski said unpleasantly. 'It is quite possible for us to get this formula without your help, but it would be as useless to us as it is to the American Government. Do I have to remind you that the formula is in code and this has proved to be unbreakable? For two years the American Government has tried to break the code. Now, they admit defeat.'

'I propose to break the code,' Radnitz said quietly. 'Nothing is impossible if you have brains and money. I have both. I am offering your people the formula decoded. In exchange for a financial consideration, you get the formula. If you are not satisfied, I don't get the money.' Radnitz regarded the glowing tip of his cigar. 'It is as simple as that. What is less simple is how much do you bid?' He glanced out of the car's window. They were driving down Karl Marx Allee with its lighted shops—the best, but still unimpressive, shopping district of East Berlin.

'You are serious?' Douzenski asked, his voice startled. 'You really mean you can break this code that has defeated all the American experts?'

'I wouldn't be wasting my time here if I wasn't serious,' Radnitz said in a bored tone. 'You don't imagine I enjoy going through your ridiculous formalities just to meet you and to see this,' and he waved to the dismal shops and the deserted streets. 'I ask again: what do you bid?'

Douzenski drew in a long breath.

'I have been instructed to tell you that we agree to pay in cash two hundred and fifty thousand dollars.' He paused, then went on, his voice rising: 'A fortune!'

Radnitz regarded the end of his cigar. He had expected such an offer. He had to restrain the white hot rage that surged through him to have to deal with such a shabby creature.

'Are you serious?' he said, repeating Douzenski's words mockingly.

Douzenski looked in his direction. He couldn't see Radnitz clearly in the dark car.

'Of course, but we will have to be satisfied it is the formula under discussion.'

'To be of any real value, the formula can only be owned by one country,' Radnitz said quietly. 'I am prepared to let your people examine the decoded formula for two days, then if you fail to pay me, I would sell a copy of the formula to another country. You understand that?'

'How do we know you wouldn't try to sell the copy after we have bought the original?' Douzenski demanded, delighted with his shrewdness.

'Because I deal with Nations,' Radnitz returned. 'When I make a bargain, I keep it.'

This Douzenski had heard and he nodded.

'So we are agreed?'

'Agreed? Did I say so? I understand you are making an offer of a quarter of a million dollars. That I can understand. Everyone makes an offer, but everyone does not make a ridiculous offer,' Radnitz said, an edge to his voice. 'Now let me tell you something, my friend. One of my agents has hinted—no more than that—to the Chinese Government that the formula ZCX, decoded, of course, could be for sale.' Radnitz paused. His hooded eyes regarded Douzenski's face, caught from time to time by the passing street lights. 'The Chinese Government know the value of the formula. Without hesitation, they have offered three million dollars. Did you hear what I said . . . three million dollars!'

Douzenski sat bolt upright.

'Three million dollars!' he gasped. 'That is absurd!'

'You think so?' Radnitz's cold contempt was now apparent both in his voice and his attitude. 'The Chinese Government don't think so.' He paused to draw on his cigar. 'Very well, then let us consider the deal is off.' Picking up the microphone, he switched it on and said to Ko-Yu, 'The Russian Embassy.'

Douzenski took a grubby handkerchief from his pocket and wiped his sweating hands.

'My Government would never pay such a sum,' he said hoarsely.

'No? Are they so poor?' Radnitz touched off the long ash from his cigar into the silver ashtray at his elbow. 'How sad. However, I don't take such a remark made by a lower civil servant—is that how you describe yourself?—seriously. Because I like the Chinese less than I like the Russians I would be prepared to make a quick deal—three and a half million dollars in cash. The formula, decoded, could be in your people's hand in three months. It would be understood that I do not get paid if I cannot supply the formula, decoded.'

'I haven't the authority,' Douzenski began feebly, but Radnitz cut him short.

'I am quite aware of that. We are now returning to your Embassy. I will leave you to make the necessary arrangements.

I will be returning to the Bristol Hotel. Send me a telegram there if your people decide they wish to buy the formula at my price.'

'I must ask you to stay the night at an hotel here,' Douzenski said, trying to regain his lost authority. 'Then I could come and see you. I am unable to come to see you at the Bristol.'

'I have no intention of staying at any of your miserable hotels,' Radnitz said as the car slowed to a stop outside the Russian Embassy. 'Send me a telegram,' and he opened the car door.

Douzenski regarded him, the brim of his shabby hat hiding the hate in his eyes, then he got out and slammed the door shut. Radnitz lowered the glass partition between himself and Ko-Yu.

'The frontier at once!'

They arrived at Checkpoint Charlie in five minutes, but that was time enough for Douzenski to have telephoned. Two fur capped guards were waiting.

The barrier was raised and the Rolls moved into the no-man's land. There was considerable delay in checking Radnitz's passport. The official seemed to be in no hurry. Radnitz waited with a number of Americans who had crossed from the West to the East to attend the opening night of the Komische Oper. He watched the Americans leave; still he waited. Finally, after a further twenty minute wait, the official stamped his papers and returned his passport. The man had a smirking grin on his fat face as he waved Radnitz away.

Radnitz, his eyes glittering with rage, returned to the Rolls. The two fur capped guards were waiting. They began to search the car while Radnitz walked up and down, trying to keep warm.

Ko-Yu came up to him, his small yellow face expressionless.

'Excuse, sir. They ask about the heater,' he said.

Radnitz walked over to the car.

'What is it?' he asked in German.

One of the guards threw the beam of his flashlight onto the big heater under the car's dashboard.

'What is this?'

'A heater.'

'We wish to see it. Have it taken down.'

'Taken down?' Radnitz's hooded eyes turned bleak. 'What do you mean? It is a heater. There is nothing concealed in it.'

'Have it taken down,' the guard repeated woodenly. 'We wish to examine it.'

Radnitz looked at Ko-Yu.

'Can you take it down?'

'Yes, sir, but it will take time.'

'Then do it,' Radnitz said and got into the car. He lit a cigar, controlling his fury, knowing he was in no-man's land and these stupid animals in their fur caps had more power than he had. Turning on the pilot light, he began to read the papers he took from his brief-case.

The two guards stood over Ko-Yu as he began to strip out the heater. Twenty minutes later, as Ko-Yu pulled off the cover of the heater, a car came through the barrier and Douzenski jumped out and came quickly to the Rolls. He waved his hand at the guards, then, opening the door of the Rolls, he slid into the seat beside Radnitz.

The guards told Ko-Yu to replace the heater cover and then walked away.

'I am sorry,' Douzenski said. The smell of his sweat made Radnitz draw more deeply on his cigar. 'This was too important. I had to delay you. We agree. We will pay three and a half million dollars for the decoded formula on the terms you have suggested.'

Radnitz continued to make notes, continued to consult the papers in his hand. For some two minutes, he worked, then he put down the papers and stared at Douzenski, his slate grey eyes burning with rage.

'I have been kept waiting in the cold for an hour,' he said. 'My time is valuable. I will not be treated in this fashion by a Communist Government. My price is now four million dollars. Telephone them! Explain that my price has risen because a stupid member of their party has dared to keep me waiting! Do you hear? Four million dollars!'

Appalled by the glittering fury in Radnitz's eyes, Douzenski backed out of the car. He ran into one of the wooden huts. Radnitz went back to reading his papers. Ko-Yu finally fixed the heater. There was a delay of fifteen minutes, then Douzenski returned. He leaned into the car. His face was the colour of tallow and sweat beads glistened on his skin.

'Yes . . . it is agreed,' he said in a flat, hopeless voice. 'Four million dollars.'

Radnitz pressed the button that raised the electrically controlled window, shutting Douzenski out. Then he said to Ko-Yu 'The Bristol.'

There was no delay when the Rolls stopped at the second barrier. The heavy, steel pole was immediately lifted and the car swept through, back into West Berlin.

Reaching the Bristol Hotel, Radnitz walked to the telephone

and Telex Bureau. He asked for a telegram form, then, writing in his thin, neat script, he composed the following:

Jonathan Lindsey.
George V Hotel. Paris 8.
Arrange meeting with C for Charlie. 13.00 hrs. Hotel. 16th.
Radnitz.

He handed the telegram to the girl operator with a DM.10 bill, then he walked across the hotel lobby to the elevator.

As the automatic doors closed and as the elevator took him swiftly to the third floor, he allowed his fat grim face to relax into a smile of triumph.

Four million dollars!

After so much thinking and planning, the prize now seemed to be within his grasp.

Alan Craig cautiously opened the door of his apartment, looked down the long corridor, listened, then stepped back.

'On your way, Jerry,' he said. 'Hurry!'

The slim, blond youth, wearing skin-tight jeans and a black wind cheater slid around Craig, gave him a sneering little grin and started down the corridor.

Craig shut the front door and walked back to the sitting-room. That had been a mistake, he told himself. He shrugged uneasily. Well, you can't always be right. This time tomorrow, he would be on the Pan-Am flight to New York. Paris would be behind him. It was time. The two months he had spent in Paris had been a little too hectic. He stood in the middle of the room, rubbing his jaw while he thought of Jerry Smith whom he had picked up in the Drug Store's arcade. During the week they had seen a lot of each other. Jerry had been amusing, willing and—Craig paused to consider it and then admitted it—exciting. But this night something had gone wrong. That sneering little grin that kept coming. Every so often Craig had caught Jerry looking at him. Could it have been contempt in those close set eyes?

Well, he was gone. He wouldn't see him again. He didn't want to see him again. Still frowning, Craig walked into the bedroom. He had better begin packing. He glanced at his gold Omega. The time was a little after eleven. He took a suitcase from the top of the wardrobe and put it on the bed.

Alan Craig was thirty-three years of age. Tall, dark with a sensitive, handsome face, good eyes and an obvious Etonian background, he had been Personal Assistant to Mervin Warren, Head of Rocket Research for the past five years. Since leaving England, and settling in the United States, Craig had had a successful career. He had gone to Washington as a junior official attached to a Rocket Research group sent over by the British Government on a fact-finding exchange of views. He had been spotted by Mervin Warren who was always on the look-out for keen, young talent. Warren had decided this brilliant young man could be more useful to him than to the London group. An offer was made and accepted, and Warren had had no regrets. He quickly satisfied himself that he had found the best and most intelligent Personal Assistant he could wish to find.

Warren had been in Paris now for two months conferring with French scientists in yet another exchange of views and ideas. Their final meeting had taken place the previous day. Tomorrow, he and Craig would be returning to Washington.

As Craig opened the suitcase, the telephone bell rang. He walked into the sitting-room and picked up the receiver.

'Yes?'

'Is that you, Alan?'

He recognized the soft voice with its strong American accent and he became alert.

'Hello there, Jon. I'm just packing. How are you?'

'Fine . . . fine. Look, Alan, could you come down to my hotel? Say in a couple of hours? I've something that will interest you. It's important.'

'Why, yes, of course. At one o'clock? What is it?'

'See you at one then,' and the line went dead.

Craig was puzzled. Something that will interest you. Was Jonathan Lindsey going to make him an offer? he wondered. Craig was ambitious. He had no intention of remaining much longer as Warren's general factotum. He had met Lindsey at an Embassy cocktail party and had immediately liked him; a man around sixty years of age, tall, white haired, ruddy complexion with steady pale blue eyes who said he was in oil. Craig knew power and money when he met the combination. He knew instinctively that Lindsey was important, and Craig was always drawn to and interested in people of importance. They had met again. Lindsey usually dined at *La Tour d'Argent,* and Craig was more than willing to eat at such a luxury restaurant at Lindsey's expense. They were quickly on first name terms. Now suddenly . . . something that will interest you.

He packed the suitcase, then changed into a grey lounge suit and slid into black, highly polished casual shoes. He surveyed himself in the full mirror, deciding he looked pale and there were dark shadows under his eyes. He grimaced. That Jerry, he thought. Paris had been too hectic . . . too many temptations. He would be glad to get back to Washington. He slapped his cheeks sharply, bringing slight colour to them. That was better, he thought. He went into the sitting-room. Should he have a drink? He felt pretty low. A shot of Vodka might set him up. He mixed a Vodka and lime juice, then sat down, nursing the drink, his mind on Lindsey.

Suppose Lindsey offered him a job? That meant Texas. Would he want to bury himself in Texas? It would depend on the money. He would play hard to get. He knew Lindsey was impressed by his record. He had seen him talking to Mervin Warren and later, Lindsey had said they had discussed him. Lindsey had looked thoughtfully at him, those pale blue eyes probing. 'Warren tells me you are the best P.A. he has ever had,' he had said finally. 'Coming from Warren that means something.'

Craig had laughed, pleased, but had waved a deprecating hand.

'Oh, I get by,' he said. 'The truth is the job really doesn't extend me. I'm looking for something I can really get my teeth into.' It was a hint . . . a seed dropped. Now, it looked as if the seed was germinating.

At exactly one o'clock, Craig got out of the taxi outside the George V Hotel. He paid off the driver, then walked into the vestibule. Not seeing Lindsey, he walked over to the concierge.

'Is Mr. Lindsey around?' he asked.

'Is it Mr. Craig?' The concierge regarded him, his head slightly on one side.

'That's right.'

'Mr. Lindsey is expecting you. Would you please go up to Suite 457 on the fourth floor, monsieur.'

A little surprised, Craig nodded and walked over to the elevator. At the fourth floor, he walked along the wide corridor until he came to a door numbered 457. He pressed the buzzer and waited.

The door was opened by a slightly built Japanese servant, wearing a white coat and black silk trousers. He bowed to Craig and stood aside.

Impressed, Craig moved into the small lobby, taking off his camel hair coat which the Japanese put on a hanger with respectful care.

'This way, monsieur,' he said and opened a door, bowing Craig into a large saloon, tastefully furnished. Over the fireplace hung a 1958 Picasso. On the overmantel stood exquisitely carved figures in green and yellow jade. On the occasional tables were gold cigarette boxes, gold lighters and onyx ashtrays. On the opposite wall, facing Craig was a Matisse. Nearby was a glass cabinet containing a collection of Ming ware, and Craig who in his spare time was a museum addict immediately recognized their enormous value. He was moving towards the cabinet when another door opened and Herman Radnitz came in, closing the door behind him.

Craig looked at the squat, fat man, startled and surprised. He felt a tremor of uneasiness as Radnitz regarded him, the slate grey eyes under their hooded lids surveying him with a bleak, searching stare.

'You are Alan Craig?' Radnitz asked in his hard guttural voice.

'Yes.'

'You may want to look at these disgusting things,' Radnitz said and handed Craig a large envelope.

Craig took the envelope, but continued to stare at Radnitz. 'I don't understand,' he said uneasily. 'I was expecting Mr. Lindsey.'

'Look at them!' Radnitz snapped. 'I have no time to waste!' He walked over to one of the occasional tables, selected a cigar, cut it carefully, then lit it. He walked over to the window and looked down at the passing traffic.

Craig looked at the envelope, lifted the flap and drew out six glossy photographic prints. One glance stopped his heartbeat for a split second, then his heart began to race and he felt icy sweat break out on his face. He shuffled through the prints, then returned them to the envelope and put the envelope down on one of the tables. His first thought was that his life had ended. He would leave the hotel, return to his apartment and kill himself. Just how he would do it, he had no idea, but he would do it.

Radnitz turned and regarded him.

'On the back of the envelope is a list of people who will be sent these photographs,' he said. 'Read it.'

Craig remained motionless, not looking at Radnitz, his face ashen, sick to his soul.

'Read it!' Radnitz said again.

Slowly, Craig picked up the envelope. Neatly typed were the names of those people who loved and respected him. His mother . . . his sister . . . his grandmother . . . Harry Matthews who had partnered him in winning the Rackets Championship at Eton . . . Father Brian Selby who had given him his first Communion . . .

John Brassey, his Oxford coach who had predicted a brilliant career for him . . . and, of course, Mervin Warren.

'I want a photograph of Formula ZCX,' Radnitz said. 'That should not be difficult. I have made your task fairly simple.' He crossed the room, opened a drawer and took from it a small camera in a soft leather zip case. 'This camera is entirely automatic. Lay the formula on a flat surface, stand immediately above it and take ten photographs. You will bring the camera containing the film to the Hilton Hotel, Washington, and give it to Mr. Lindsey. When he is satisfied the photographs are in order, he will give you the negatives of these disgusting things and all the copies. Is that understood? If you fail, copies of this filth will be mailed to the people listed on the envelope.'

'How—how did you get these—photos?' Craig asked in a husky whisper.

Radnitz shrugged.

'Your friend, Jerry Smith, is one of the many creatures I have to employ. Take the camera and leave me.'

'The formula is useless,' Craig said desperately. 'Everyone knows that. You are forcing me to . . .'

'You will be at the Hilton Hotel a week from today . . . the 26th,' Radnitz said. 'If you don't have the photographs of the formula . . .' He shrugged and left the room.

Craig stood still, clutching the camera. He remained like that until Ko-Yu came into the room with his coat. Then he picked up the envelope, snatched his coat from the Japanese servant and hurriedly left the hotel.

Jonathan Lindsey had been Radnitz's Chief of Operations for the past ten years. He drew a salary of $100,000 a year, and earned every dollar of it. Although he was sixty years of age, he kept himself in first class trim. He was tall and lean, a non-drinker and a non-smoker, and he had a nimble, shrewd brain and a soulless mind. Suave, smooth, with perfect manners, he frequented the Embassies of the world, and was on friendly and even familiar terms with several of the crowned heads of Europe. As a front man, he was invaluable to Radnitz who preferred to keep in the background. Whenever there was an important operation, Radnitz gave his instructions, and Lindsey carried them out with unfailing success.

It was fortunate for Lindsey that he liked luxury hotels for he spent his entire life moving from one hotel to another, crossing the Atlantic sometimes as often as three times a week, visiting

European cities to fix up a deal here and a merger there, staying at the best hotels where he was known to be a big spender and always received immediate and excellent service.

On the afternoon of October 26th, Lindsey was sitting in the foyer of the Washington Hilton Hotel, watching the busy scene, relaxed, his well shaped hands folded in his lap, his pale blue eyes regarding the men and women who came and went, speculating on who they were and what they did for a living. Lindsey was always interested in people, no matter how rich or poor they might be.

A few minutes to three o'clock, he saw Alan Craig enter the hotel and look around, hesitating. He got slowly to his feet and crossed the foyer, his charming smile lighting up his face, thinking how bad Craig looked. The stupid fellow couldn't have been sleeping well, Lindsey thought. Well, that was not surprising. If you led the life Craig led, sooner or later, there had to be a blow-back.

'Hello, Alan,' he said in his soft cultured voice. He made no offer to shake hands. 'Punctual as always. Let us go upstairs.'

Craig looked at him, his face drawn and set. Wordlessly, he followed Lindsey to the elevator, rode up with him to the third floor and followed him along the corridor to Lindsey's suite.

'I hope you were successful,' Lindsey said as he closed the door.

Still saying nothing, Craig took the camera in its leather case from his pocket and handed it to Lindsey.

'Sit down. I won't be long. Do you want a drink?'

Craig shook his head and sat down.

'Excuse me. I will be as quick as I can,' and Lindsey left the room. He entered the bathroom. Here, he had a developing tank, the chemicals mixed and a red safe light installed. Working with quick efficiency, he developed the film, fixed it, washed it, then turning on the overhead light, he examined the negative with a powerful magnifying glass.

These Japanese cameras are really remarkable, he thought as he studied the needle sharp negatives. Satisfied, he hung the strip of film up to dry and returned to the sitting-room.

Craig looked at him, his face white and haggard.

'Perfectly satisfactory,' Lindsey said, then unlocking a drawer in his desk, he took out a thick envelope and handed it to Craig. 'The bargain is completed, I think.'

Craig peered into the envelope. He saw the negatives and the prints.

'How do I know you haven't kept copies?' he demanded, his eyes desperately searching Lindsey's calm face.

'My dear boy, you should know me better than that,' Lindsey said quietly. 'A bargain is a bargain. I don't cheat.'

Craig hesitated, then nodded wretchedly.

'Yes . . . I'm sorry.' He paused, then went on, 'The formula is useless. I—I wouldn't have given it to you if I thought the code could be broken. It can't! Do you hear? It is useless! It can't be broken!'

'So I understand,' Lindsey said mildly. 'Well, never mind. My principal wants it. What he does with it is no concern of ours. We now have it. You have what you want, and the matter is concluded. Thank you.'

Craig stared at him, then, snatching up the envelope, he went quickly from the room.

Lindsey walked over to the telephone.

'Is Mr. Silk there, please?' he asked the operator.

'Yes, sir. One moment, sir.'

There was a moment's delay, then a voice said, 'Silk.'

'He's on his way down now,' Lindsey said.

'Okay.'

Craig had to wait a few minutes before a taxi pulled up outside the hotel. He waited until the fare had paid off the driver then climbed into the taxi, giving his apartment address. His mind was in too much of a turmoil for him to notice two well dressed men slide into a Ford Thunderbird and follow his taxi.

The driver of the Thunderbird was around twenty-six years of age. His name was Chet Keegan. He had a baby faced handsomeness, blond, longish hair, a small thin mouth and close set green eyes. His companion was some fifteen years older, a hatchet faced man with a glass eye and a white scar running down the side of his left cheek. His name was Lu Silk. These two men were vicious and dangerous thugs: professional killers who would tackle any job, any kind of danger, any kind of killing if the money was right. They were soulless robots who obeyed Lindsey's commands, not thinking, not questioning, knowing from long experience that Lindsey's scale of pay easily topped any other offer they might receive.

Unaware that he was being followed, Craig relaxed back in the taxi and looked at the photographs he had taken from the envelope. He shuddered. Even if he had had the guts to kill himself, he knew that the hurt and the horror these photographs would have caused the people they could have been sent to were too appalling to contemplate. Well, he now had them back. He trusted Lindsey. A bargain was a bargain, Lindsey had said. Never again! Craig vowed to himself. Never again would he pick up a stranger. He had no need to. He had plenty of friends whom he could trust. That had been a moment of utter madness, and how he had paid for it!

The actual photographing of the formula had presented no difficulties or incurred any risk. By now, Mervin Warren had complete trust in Craig, and left him to lock the Top Security safe and to clear up, often leaving him alone in the building. It was a mere matter of a few minutes to take the ten photographs and return the formula to the safe. But Craig's conscience nagged at him. He kept assuring himself that the code was unbreakable. Yet why had this man blackmailed him to get these photographs? Was it possible that there was a means of breaking the code? Craig felt cold sweat on his face. He knew the vital importance of the formula. He knew every American code expert had tried in vain during the past two years to break it. He knew if the code could be broken and the metal produced, it would mean the biggest and quickest breakthrough in rocket development that could be imagined. But if the Russians broke the code . . . !

He wiped his face with his handkerchief. Such thinking was ridiculous, he told himself. No one could break the code . . . that was for sure!

The taxi pulled up outside his apartment block and he paid off the driver. He didn't notice the black Thunderbird as it drew up some distance away, nor did he notice the two well dressed men as they got out of the car.

He rode up in the elevator to the fifth floor, unlocked his front door, entered and shut the door. He took off his coat, then moving through his well furnished sitting-cum-dining-room, he went into the kitchen where he found an empty biscuit tin. His one thought now was to burn the photographs and the negatives. As he carried the tin into the sitting-room he told himself he would have to be careful . . . one photograph at a time. He mustn't make too much smoke.

As he put the biscuit tin down on the table, the front doorbell rang.

He stiffened, his eyes alarmed. For a moment he hesitated, then rushed the tin back into the kitchen. Returning to the sitting-room, he pushed the bulky envelope of photographs under a chair cushion.

The bell rang again. He went reluctantly to the door and opened it.

Lu Silk put the barrel of his Mauser with its cone shaped silencer against Craig's chest and rode him back into the lobby.

'No fuss,' Silk said softly. 'This rod makes no noise. It could blow your chest apart.'

Craig stared into the bleak, scarred face and into the black single eye. The glass eye looked more human than the live one. He felt sudden terror, a paralysing wave of fear run through him. He was vaguely aware of a second man who came in and closed the front door.

'What—what do you want?' he asked hoarsely as Silk continued to ride him back across the small lobby and into the sitting-room.

'Plenty of time,' Silk said. 'Just behave.'

They were in the sitting-room now. Keegan pulled an upright chair from the dining table and set it in the middle of the room.

'Sit down,' Silk said.

Craig sat on the chair. Terror made his muscles twitch. He tried frantically to control the twitching but without success.

Silk asked, 'Where are the photos?'

Craig stared at him in horror.

'But you can't . . . Lindsey said . . .' He stopped as Silk's single eye gleamed red with contained, savage fury. Hopelessly, he pointed to the chair. Keegan lifted the cushion, found the envelope, glanced inside, then nodded to Silk.

Silk moved a few steps back. He looked at Keegan, his scarred face expressionless. Keegan moved quickly. He flicked out a length of nylon cord from his pocket, stepped behind Craig, dropped a noose over Craig's head and around his neck. Then he dropped flat on his back in a Judo fall, hauling on the cord. The movement was done in a split second.

Craig felt the cord bite into his flesh. He went over backwards with a crash. Keegan slammed his feet on Craig's shoulders, hauling on the cord.

Silk unscrewed the silencer on his gun, dropped the silencer into his pocket, then returned the gun to its holster. By the time he had done this, Craig was dead.

Keegan got to his feet while Silk took the photographs from the envelope. He selected one which he put on an occasional table. The rest he returned to the envelope which he forced into his overcoat pocket. In the meantime, Keegan had gone into the bathroom. Now, he returned.

'There's a hook on the door strong enough to take him,' he said.

The two men caught hold of Craig's lifeless body and dragged it into the bathroom. They hung it by the cord from the hook. Craig's polished shoes just touched the tiled floor.

They regarded him, then Silk nodded.

'A nice clean job,' he said. 'Let's go.'

Keegan opened the front door, looked along the corridor, listened, then jerked his head.

The two men rode down in the elevator.

No one saw them leave. No one noticed the Thunderbird as it drifted through the heavy traffic back to the Washington Hilton Hotel.

Jean Rodin, Radnitz's Paris agent, was short, middle-aged, fat and balding. He had a perpetual smile which never reached his glassy, expressionless eyes. He handled Radnitz's affairs in France intelligently and efficiently. Many of the things Radnitz required him to do were criminal. Rodin was a careful man. He never made a mistake. The money Radnitz paid him was impressive. He was one of Radnitz's most reliable agents.

He received a cable from Washington on the afternoon of Craig's death. The cable was brief and to the point:

Rodin
Hotel Maurice. Paris 6.
Smith. Complete operation.
Lindsey.

He lit a Gauloise cigarette, put on his hat and overcoat and went down to where he had parked his Simca car. He drove with the heavy traffic until he reached Quai des Grands Augustins where after some difficulty he found a parking place. He walked down Rue Seguier, turned into a dirty courtyard and entered a shabby apartment block. He climbed to the sixth floor, pausing every now and then to regain his breath.

Rodin adored food and smoked forty cigarettes a day. Any form of exercise distressed him, and stair climbing was his least happy experience. Finally, he reached the sixth floor and knocked on a door.

Jerry Smith, wearing a dirty singlet and skin-tight jeans, opened the door, a scowl on his face, but seeing Rodin, he brightened.

'Hello, Mr. Rodin, I didn't expect you. Got some more work for me?'

Rodin regarded him with disgust. Such creatures had to be

used, he told himself, but to have contact with them made him feel soiled.

'I think I can find you something.' He spoke English with a strong French accent. He moved into the small, disgustingly dirty room.

'I did a good job, didn't I?' Jerry went on, grinning. 'I should have been paid more. How about it, Mr. Rodin?'

Rodin regarded him. They always wanted more money and sooner or later they always talked.

'Yes, perhaps.' He put his hand inside his overcoat. His small, fat fingers closed over the butt of a ·25 automatic. He knew Jerry Smith lived alone on this floor and the old lady who lived below was stone deaf. He could hear the roar of the traffic as it pounded along the Quai. It would be safe to shoot.

As Jerry Smith edged forward, greed in his eyes, Rodin drew the gun and shot him through the heart. The brittle bang of the small gun mingled with the roar of the traffic and was lost.

Rodin walked out onto the landing, pushing the gun back into its holster. He closed the door and made his way without hurrying down the stairs and to his car.

Back at his hotel, he sent the following cable.

Lindsey, Washington Hilton Hotel
Operation completed.
Rodin.

Radnitz had told Lindsey to leave no dangerous loose ends.

Lindsey believed in being thorough. What were two lives worth against a four million dollar take?

The Belvedere Hotel is considered the most expensive and the most luxurious hotel in Florida. Situated on the magnificent bay that half circles Paradise City, it is the favourite resting place for the Texas oil men, movie stars and anyone with more than a half a million dollar income.

Radnitz rented the penthouse suite at the hotel on a year-to-year basis. Fifteen storeys above the sand and the sea, the penthouse suite consisted of three bedrooms, three bathrooms, a deluxe kitchen, two fine reception rooms, a smaller room used by Radnitz's secretary and a vast terrace complete with a swimming pool, awnings, a cocktail bar, lounging chairs and tropical flowers.

Whenever Radnitz was planning a big operation, he retired to the penthouse as he thought better, planned better when in the direct blaze of Florida's sun.

He was sitting on the terrace, wearing a white towelling shirt and blue linen slacks, a cigar in his mouth, a highball at his elbow when Lindsey crossed the red and white tiles and pulled up a chair and sat down.

Radnitz, his hooded eyes a little sleepy, raised his eyebrows. 'Did you get it?'

Lindsey handed over a big envelope.

'No loose ends?' Radnitz asked as he drew out several big prints of the formula.

'No loose ends,' Lindsey said quietly.

Knowing Lindsey, Radnitz didn't waste time asking for details. He studied the formula, then returned the prints to the envelope which he put on the table.

'Odd to think this could be worth four million dollars,' he said, reflectively, 'but as it is, it is worthless.'

Lindsey didn't say anything. When he was with Radnitz, he seldom talked, except to answer questions. He had an enormous repect for this fat, squat man, knowing him to be one of the most powerful and brilliant financial geniuses, who had built his kingdom from nothing, relying on his brains, his ruthlessness and a built-in instinct that led him unerringly to where big money was to be found.

'I am told Alan Craig committed suicide,' Radnitz said, not looking at Lindsey, his hooded eyes studying a group of girls in bikinis, disporting themselves on the beach far below him. 'Sad . . .'

'Yes,' Lindsey said. 'The police found an incriminating photo in his apartment. It is being hushed up. Warren has thrown a blanket over it all.'

'Just as well.' Radnitz sipped his drink. 'Well, now, we can start the operation. You have a lot to do. First, let me put you in the picture. I want you to know exactly what you have to do. I have put my own ideas down on paper. They may or may not be helpful. You have the ultimate decision on every move. I am leaving for Prague. There is a deal there coming up that could be interesting. From Prague, I go to Hong Kong. They are, as usual, short of water. There is some question of building another reservoir in the New Territories. I have an option on the contract, but a reservoir is useless without water. From Hong Kong, I go to Pekin. I hope to persuade the Chinese Government to fill the reservoir. I will be back in ten weeks.' He stared at Lindsey, the slate grey eyes cold. 'I expect you to have broken the code by then.'

Lindsey crossed one long leg over the other and regarded his glossy black shoe. His face remained expressionless.

'There is only one man who can decode the formula,' Radnitz went on after a long pause: 'The man who invented it. His name is Paul Forrester. He not only invented the formula, but also the code. Let me tell you about the formula. It is for a new and entirely revolutionary metal. From what I hear, this metal is ten times lighter than steel and three times as durable. It is also completely friction proof. Using this metal, it will be possible to make a Moon shot half as cheaply as before. It is obviously the ideal metal for any kind of space rocket. Nothing like it has ever been thought of before. As you probably know the inventor, Paul Forrester, is now in the Harrison Wentworth Asylum. It is a private asylum for the very rich. The American Government have put him there in the hope that he will recover and give them the key to the formula. He has been there now for twenty-six months. He is quite unco-operative, spending his days staring into space, suspicious of everyone, not reacting to treatment . . . in fact, a zombie.' Radnitz paused, then after another sip at his highball, went on, 'You may well ask yourself why this man is in an asylum. Without doubt he is one of the best and most impressive scientists in the world. I have had his background investigated. It seems he has always been an odd man out. His father committed suicide. His mother went off with some man and disappeared. Forrester was brought up by a spinster aunt, a sour, disillusioned woman who did her duty, but no more. Forrester was brilliant at school with a genius for mathematics. But he was unpopular, a loner and an introvert. I won't bother you with his success at school or at Harvard. At the age of thirty-three, he was appointed Chief Scientist at the Paradise City Rocket Research Station. His assistant did all the routine work. Forrester had his own laboratory and no one knew what he was working on. For those who had the insight, signs of manic-depression were beginning to show: irritability, sleeplessness, suspicion, restlessness and so on.

'Before taking up his post here, he married an utterly unsuitable woman as so often men of his brilliance will marry. This woman—I don't need to bother you with details about her—was the ultimate cause of his mental breakdown.

'Getting back to his work, he had a lab assistant, a young woman whose name is Nona Jacey. She is important. She was the only person allowed in his laboratory. Her duties were simple. She merely kept the place clean, answered the telephone, kept unwelcome visitors away, brought Forrester his lunch. I will come back to her in a moment.

'The Medical Officer on the Research Station began to get worried about Forrester. He was sure Forrester was heading for a breakdown and he alerted Warren in Washington. Warren had heard that Forrester was working on something important, but had no idea what it was. When he got the doctor's report, he became alarmed. He sent for Forrester. He arranged for a top psychiatrist to be present at the meeting. He got nothing from Forrester who refused to say what he was working on. Another interview was arranged for the following day. When Forrester had returned to his hotel, the psychiatrist said bluntly that Forrester was on the verge of a mental crack-up . . . all the signs were there. Before Warren could make up his mind what to do, Forrester had packed and had returned to the Research Station.' Radnitz paused again to sip his drink. 'He caught his wife in bed with his assistant, about the only man on the Research Station he had any contact with. He killed the man and was only just prevented from killing his wife. He was found battering down the bathroom door, quite insane and extremely violent. The killing, his wife's behaviour and Forrester's insanity were hushed up. It became a Top Secret secret. Warren arranged for Forrester to be put in the Harrison Wentworth Asylum. There he remains, quiet, moody . . . a zombie.'

Lindsey recrossed his legs.

'What makes you think he will decode the formula?' he asked.

'You will read my suggestions later,' Radnitz said. 'I have talked to a number of mental specialists. There is a chance. As regards the code it is apparently simple but without a key, unbreakable. What Forrester seems to have done is to substitute words and numbers for other words and numbers, probably taken from some book. Every book in his home and laboratory has been examined without finding any of them marked. This isn't surprising as Forrester has a remarkable photographic memory . . . quite a freak thing. He is or rather was able to read a page of print and then recite it back without making a single error. So it would seem the key to the code is in his head.'

Lindsey thought the girl running across the sands to the sea in the far distance shouldn't be wearing a bikini. Although her figure was acceptable, her thighs were enormously fat . . . so fat, she ran awkwardly.

'This girl . . . Nona Jacey?' he asked, shifting his eyes back to Radnitz.

'Yes. She is still working at the Research Station in some lowly job. It was she who gave Warren the clue about this metal. Forrester liked and trusted her . . . this is important. She had no idea he was a mental case. She has been interrogated by the top scientists, the C.I.A. and by Warren. From the interrogation comes the fact that Forrester had discovered this metal. She was present when he hit on the formula and he told her about it. She was puzzled and worried when he said no one should have it. He was alarmingly elated and told her the United States did not deserve the fruits of his brain. It was thought that he hadn't discovered anything of importance and all this talk was part of his growing madness, but the girl is emphatic she has seen the metal and has seen the various tests Forrester made . . . if one is to believe her, the metal exists. A thorough search for the metal was made, but Forrester either has hidden it or destroyed it and it was never found. As you know, every effort has been made to break the code without success. So the affair stands . . . stalemate. Nona Jacey is vitally important. You will see what I suggest.' He looked inquiringly at Lindsey. 'Any questions?'

'A lot,' Lindsey said, 'but I want to read your suggestions first.'

'Yes, do that,' Radnitz said. 'You will find them on my desk. This is probably one of my most important operations. If you run into any major difficulties, you may consult me. I am relying on you,' and with a wave of his hand, he dismissed Lindsey, then sank lower in his chair and stared out at the beach and the blue sea, glittering in the sunshine.

CHAPTER TWO

As THE HANDS of the wall clock pointed to 5.30, Nona Jacey hastily cleared her desk, slapped the cover over her typewriter and got hurriedly to her feet.

The two other typists watched her with mischievous grins.

'Don't break your neck, honey,' the plump one said. 'No man's worth that.'

Nona winked.

'This one is,' she said and hurried out of the office, down the corridor to the staff changing-room. As she washed her hands, she hummed happily under her breath. She paused to run a comb through her hair, put a touch of powder on her nose, regarded herself for a brief moment in the mirror, then leaving the building she hurried over to the car park.

At the age of twenty-five, Nona Jacey was attractive without being beautiful, tall, well built, with auburn hair, sea green eyes and a *retrousseé* nose. It was now over two years since she had worked for Paul Forrester. His memory had faded, although from time to time she thought of him. Her present job, secretary to an Assistant Scientist, was dull, and she often thought of the excitement and interest she had experienced while working for Forrester. But all that was so much water under the bridge. She was in love. Three months ago she had met at a cocktail party a tall Gregory Peck type of young man who was the star reporter on the *Paradise Herald,* the leading City daily. His name was Alec Sherman. They had taken one look at each other, human chemicals had begun to work and they had known immediately they were meant for each other. This day was Alec's birthday, and Nona had invited him to dinner. This would be the first time he had been to her two room apartment, and the first time he was to sample her cooking of which she was justly proud. It would be a rush as she had to get back to the City, ten miles from the Research Station, buy the ingredients for the meal, get back to her apartment, cook the meal, change and be ready when he arrived at half past seven.

She slid into her Austin-Cooper, started the engine and drove to the barrier.

Seeing her coming, the guard lifted the steel pole and gave her a dashing salute. Nona was popular at the Station. She waved back, smiling, then headed down the highway towards the City's centre.

At this time the traffic was heavy and Nona impatiently jumped the lanes, trying to get ahead of two cars which seemed to be in no hurry. She succeeded, then moving into the fast lane, she put her foot down hard on the gas pedal.

She didn't notice the black Thunderbird parked in a lay-by, but the driver of the car had noticed her.

'There she goes,' Keegan said, started the engine and slid the big car into the line of traffic causing one driver to brake violently and curse at the top of his voice. With a show of expert driving, Keegan moved from one lane to the other until the Thunderbird caught up with the Cooper.

'She's going like a bat out of hell,' Silk said, his hat resting on the back of his head. 'These kid drivers are crazy.'

'She doesn't drive so badly,' Keegan returned. 'She's got the knack. I can tell. I'd like to see how she would handle this job.'

Silk grunted. He had no patience with the young.

In a very short while Nona reached the outskirts of the City and promptly reduced speed. She had already had several lectures from traffic cops who seemed to take a delight in leaning into her tiny car, gazing at her indignant face and holding her up while they expounded on the safe limits of speed. It would be disastrous, she told herself, if she were held up now, so she drove down the main street at a sedate thirty miles an hour with the Thunderbird a few yards behind her.

Signalling, she turned right into the parking lot of the Paradise Self-Service store. Leaving her car, she hurried into the nearby store.

The menu for the evening was to be fried oysters, wrapped in bacon, followed by sweet pepper stew, a Hungarian dish of lamb, paprika, potatos, tomatoes, stock, wine, caraway seeds, onions, salt and pepper: a dish that Nona considered to be her masterpiece.

It was while she was selecting a boned shoulder of lamb that a blond man with a small thin mouth and close set green eyes lurched into her. She staggered and turned indignantly.

'Excuse me,' the man said, tipping his hat. 'I guess I slipped,' and he moved on, disappearing into the crowd.

Nona looked at the assistant who was serving her.

'Well! Did you see? He nearly knocked me over!'

The assistant, young and admiring, grinned at her.

'What are you grumbling about, miss? You always knock me over every time I see you.'

Nona laughed.

'Oh, well . . . I'll have that one. Please be quick . . . I'm in a hurry.'

On the other side of the store, Tom Friendly, the store detective, sat on a packing case, resting his throbbing corns. He knew he should be on the floor. His job was to be constantly circling, keeping his eyes open for light fingered customers, but the noise, the heat and the fact he had been on his feet now for four hours persuaded him he should take a little rest.

He was dozing happily when a hard finger tapped his fat shoulder. He started up guiltily and stared at the tall man bending over him. This man had a glass eye and a scar running down the side of his face.

'You the dick here?' the tall man asked.

'That's me . . . what's up?' Friendly asked, trying to gather his wits together.

'There's a girl out there who's helping herself,' the tall man said. 'I thought you'd be interested. She's just visited the costume jewellery counter. She has a nice, smooth action.'

'The hell she has!' Friendly exclaimed. 'Where is she?'

'At the bacon counter,' the tall man said. 'You can't miss her. A red-head wearing a white dust coat over a blue dress.'

'You come along and point her out,' Friendly said. 'You'll be needed as a witness. You saw her take the stuff.'

The tall man smiled.

'And what were *you* doing? No . . . you saw her take the stuff. That way you get the credit,' and turning, he walked away, quickly mingling with the crowd.

Friendly hesitated, then made his way as fast as his flat feet could take him to the bacon counter.

Nona had completed her shopping. She went through the turnstile, paying for what she had bought, then carrying her purchases in two big paper sacks, she half walked, half ran to her car.

As she was putting the sacks on the back seat, she felt a tap on her shoulder. She looked around, startled.

She found herself looking at Tom Friendly's red, beery face. His little eyes were cop hard. Her startled expression gave him the impression of guilty fear.

'Let's go back to the store, miss,' he said and put a hot, sweaty hand on her arm.

Indignant, Nona tried to shake off his grip, but he tightened it.

'Let go of me!' she exclaimed. 'Let go at once!'

'I'm the store detective, miss,' Friendly said. 'Do you come quietly or do I call a cop?'

Patrolman Tom O'Brien had walked into the car park for his usual look around. There was an automatic Coke machine just inside the parking lot which he patronized around this time. O'Brien, a hefty, elderly Irishman, found sidewalk-pounding a thirsty job. He reckoned to consume fifteen Cokes on his beat, and this stop would be his tenth. He saw Friendly talking to a red-head, his hand on her arm, and he decided to see what it was all about. He and Friendly got along well together. It looked as if Friendly had picked up yet another shop-lifter.

'What's going on?' he boomed as he came to a halt before Nona.

'Tell this man to let go of me!' Nona exclaimed. In spite of her anger, she was beginning to feel a little scared.

'The old business, Tim,' Friendly said. 'She's been helping herself. Let's get her inside.'

'Come on, baby,' O'Brien said, 'and we'll get it all sorted out.'

'Im in a hurry . . . I can't . . . I . . .' Nona stammered. 'You've no right . . .'

'I said come on,' O'Brien growled. 'Let's go.'

Her face flushed, her eyes flashing, Nona hesitated, then walked with the patrolman and Friendly back to the store. She saw people were staring at her and she became flustered and embarrassed. She would sue them! she told herself. She would make them sorry for this! She would sue and sue and sue!

The manager of the store was a thin, sour faced man who regarded her with bored indifference.

'Seen taking goods from the costume jewellery counter,' Friendly announced.

The manager regarded Friendly with a jaundiced eye. He was far from satisfied with Friendly's work and was considering getting rid of him.

'You saw her?' he asked acidly.

Friendly hesitated for a brief moment, then nodded.

'Yeah . . . I saw her.'

'That's not true!' Nona exclaimed. 'I've been nowhere near the jewellery counter!'

'Would you mind turning out your pockets, miss?' the manager asked.

'I've nothing in my pockets . . . this is absurd,' and Nona plunged her hands into the two pouch pockets of her dust coat, then felt a cold chill run up her spine. Her fingers encountered what could only be bracelets and rings. She felt them, feeling the blood drain out of her face. 'There's a mistake . . . I—I never put them there . . . I . . .'

The manager's bored, sour face became even more bored.

'Let's see what you've taken,' he said. 'Come on now. Don't look so surprised, miss. It doesn't cut any ice with me.'

Slowly, Nona took from her pockets five cheap bracelets, three rings fitted with cutglass stones to look like diamonds and an imitation amber bead necklace. She dropped the articles on the manager's desk, shuddering.

'I didn't take them! Someone put them in my pocket! I swear I didn't take them!'

The manager turned to Patrolman O'Brien.

'We'll be making a charge, officer. You'll need this stuff as evidence. Can I leave it to you?'

'Sure,' O'Brien said. He scooped up the cheap jewellery and dropped it into his pocket. 'That's okay, Mr. Manawitz. Headquarters will be in touch with you.' He dropped a heavy hand on Nona's arm. 'Come on, baby. Let's go.'

'I want to telephone,' Nona said, trying to steady her voice.

'You can do all the telephoning you want when we get to the Station House,' O'Brien said. 'Come on. Move with the feet.'

The reason why all Lindsey's operations were crowned with success lay in the fact that he acquired every scrap of necessary information before planning his campaign. He was painstakingly thorough, and when he briefed the men who worked under him, he supplied them with a mass of details that made their work comparatively simple.

To obtain this information, he employed a Detective Agency staffed by ex-detectives, mainly men who had been kicked off the Force because of corruption and malpractice, but who were trained in their job and were experts in digging up any required information.

Four days before Nona's arrest, Lindsey had turned three snoopers from the Agency on to the task of digging up every scrap of information they could find regarding Nona's background and her way of life.

By tapping her telephone and shadowing her during these four days, they turned in a comprehensive report. Lindsey learned about Alec Sherman, that Nona was planning a birthday party, that Sherman was expected at her apartment at seven-thirty and she always did her shopping at the Paradise Self-Service store. He then turned two other snoopers to dig into Alec Sherman's background and their report made him thoughtful.

To Silk, he said, 'This guy Sherman could be a trouble-maker. Newspaper men are dangerous. He is crazy about the girl and he could gum up the works. Let's get him out of the way for a couple of weeks. By that time, he won't be able to make trouble.'

Silk nodded.

'I've got the photo. Leave him to me.'

On the evening of the planned birthday party, the black Thunderbird was parked some forty yards away on the opposite side of the street from Nona's apartment block. It had arrived at 7.15 p.m., and in the car both Silk and Keegan were smoking, sitting silent and relaxed.

At 7.28, a steel grey Pontiac Le Mans Sports Coupe pulled up outside the apartment block.

Keegan tossed away his cigarette.

'Here he is,' he said softly.

They watched a tall, powerfully built man get out of the car, slam the door shut and then run up the steps of the building.

Alec Sherman was telling himself that this was going to be a night that would mark a milestone in his life. He eased open the door and walked into the dimly lit lobby that smelt faintly of cabbage water and floor polish. He carried in his pocket an engagement ring with a glittering diamond that he could ill afford, set in a blue velvet lined, leather covered box. He had shopped around, and with the help of a friend, had finally come down on this diamond, being assured it was a bargain at the price, and a diamond no girl could resist.

He started up the stairs to the third floor, and he wondered, with male interest, what he was going to eat. Nona had told him she could cook, but Sherman had been around. Before meeting and falling in love with her, he had had plenty of girl-friends who had always told him the same story. When the proof was on the table, he invariably wished he had taken the girl out to a restaurant. But he had a lot of confidence in Nona. Even if she did dish up a burnt offering, he would still want to marry her. There was that thing about her that set his blood on fire, his heart thumping, and he now couldn't imagine life without her.

He rapped on the door on the third floor. While waiting, he fingered his tie and readjusted the set of his jacket. Then, puzzled, he rapped again. Still the door remained unopened. He discovered a bell push and jabbed it with his thumb. He heard the bell ringing. He stepped back and again waited. He repeated this action for the next three minutes, then it dawned on him there was no one in the apartment.

He consulted his strap watch. The time was now 7.40. Maybe she had been held up at the Research Station. She couldn't have met with an accident? Alarm jogged his mind. He went down the stairs, two at the time, to the ground floor. A sign with an arrow pointing to a door read:

Mrs. Ethel Watson. Proprietor.

He hesitated, then walked to the door and rang the bell. The door was opened by a small, bird-like woman with cold, unfriendly eyes, a tight mouth and her thinning hair done up in a bun on the top of her head. She wore a black, shapeless dress that had seen a lot of wear, and in spite of the heat, a grubby white shawl over her shoulders. She regarded Sherman without interest. In a waspish voice, she asked, 'Well, young man . . . what do you want?'

'I've just been up to Miss Jacey's apartment,' Sherman said. 'We had a date for seven-thirty. She isn't in.'

'I can't help that, can I?' Mrs. Watson said. 'If she isn't in, she isn't in.'

'I was wondering if you had heard if she had been delayed.'

Mrs. Watson screwed up her bitter mouth.

'No one tells me anything.'

Sherman realized he was wasting time. The next move would be to telephone the Research Station. It was more than possible Nona had had to work late.

'Thanks . . . sorry to have troubled you,' he said and walked across the lobby, opened the front door and ran down the steps.

He slid under the driving wheel of the Pontiac. As he was about to press down on the starter, Keegan, hiding on the floor of the back of the car, rose up and hit him behind his right ear with a sand-filled cosh.

Sherman fell forward, unconscious. Keegan knew just how hard it was necessary to hit a man to render him unconscious and just how hard to kill him. He rolled Sherman's inert body away from the driving seat so that his body slumped half on the passenger's seat, half on the car's floor. Then he climbed over the seat, slid under the driving wheel and set the car in motion.

Silk started the Thunderbird, following the Pontiac that moved at a leisurely speed to the main street. It turned right, the Thunderbird following. It drove down a narrow street and slowed as it came to a vacant building site, high with weeds and coarse grass.

The two cars stopped. Silk looked up and down the deserted street, then got out of the Thunderbird to help Keegan drag Sherman's unconscious body out of the Pontiac. Swiftly, they half carried, half dragged him into the thick, high growing weeds.

'Watch it . . . don't kill him,' Silk said. 'Just bust him up for a nice two-week stay in hospital.'

'Sure, I know,' Keegan said, and as Silk returned to the Thunderbird, he swung his foot back and kicked Sherman viciously in the face.

Silk got into the car. He glanced at his watch, saw the time was a few minutes to eight o'clock. He tilted his hat over his nose and closed his eye.

Some minutes later, Keegan came through the weeds, pausing every now and then to wipe his shoes on the rough grass, then he slid under the driving wheel.

'He's fine,' he said as he started the engine. 'He'll be as troublesome as an ant for the next two weeks. Where now?'

Silk knew and admired Keegan's expertise. Keegan could kick a man to within a heartbeat of death, and yet the man could still survive although he would be nothing to get worked up about after the beating.

'Where now?' he repeated, pushing his hat to the back of his head. 'The City Court. You leave me there. No need for both of us to check this. The Magistrate sits at nine o'clock. I'll get a taxi back.'

'Anything you say,' Keegan said and sent the Thunderbird shooting down the dark street.

At ten o'clock, Silk walked into the Belvedere Hotel, entered the elevator and was whisked up to the penthouse suite. Here, he found Lindsey on the terrace, looking down at the bright lights far below and at the young people still bathing in the warm, moonlit sea.

Lindsey turned as he heard Silk come across the red and white tiles.

'Well?'

'Just the way you wanted it,' Silk said. 'Very smooth: no trouble. She drew a week in the Pen and a twenty-five dollar fine. The Magistrate was a fat old queer who hates girls. He took one look at her and threw the book at her.'

'Sherman?'

'He didn't know what hit him. Right now, he's in the State Hospital: fractured jaw, four broken ribs and a beautiful concussion. He'll survive but it will take time.'

Lindsey winced. He hated violence, but when working for Radnitz, he had found he had to live with it.

'You've done well.' He looked down at the screaming, happy crowd on the beach. He envied them. How uncomplicated were their lives! 'This girl . . . find out when she'll be released and pick her up. Get someone to go to her apartment, pack her things and settle her rent . . . use a woman.'

'I'll take care of it,' Silk said and looked expectantly at Lindsey. 'Anything else?'

'Not right now.'

Lindsey took a roll of $50 bills from his hip pocket and handed it to Silk.

'The big operation gets going when we have the girl,' he said. 'I'll go over the details with you at the end of the week.'

'Okay.' Silk examined the roll of bills, nodded his satisfaction, then left the penthouse suite.

Lindsey wandered to the terrace balcony and looked down at the young people, splashing in the sea. He watched them for several minutes, then leaving the terrace, he entered Radnitz's study. He sat down at the desk and began to re-read the notes Radnitz had left him. When Lindsey had an operation in his lap, he concentrated his whole mind on it. This was the trickiest operation he had been given. It involved a madman and four million dollars. For the first time since he had worked for Radnitz, he wondered uneasily if he would succeed.

Sheila Latimer was Keegan's slave.

The previous summer, she had been the runner up for a Miss Florida competition, and would have won it had she been willing to have slept with two or three of the judges.

Chet Keegan was fond of young, well built girls. When he wasn't working with Silk, he was roaming around, looking for likely material to corrupt.

Any local beauty competition was his happy hunting ground. He had regarded Sheila Latimer with approval. She was tall, beautifully built, blonde with big blue eyes and full curved, red lips. What he didn't realize was that she was not only a virgin, but frightened of sex.

He found her drinking a Coke in a small bar that was at the moment empty except for the girl and the bartender. She was trying to console herself that she really could have been Miss Florida had the other creature who had won the title been less corrupt.

Keegan joined her. He had a very easy and deceptive manner with women. His handsomeness, his smooth manner, his confidence intrigued her. When he told her that she was his pick of all the girls who had been on parade, she naturally warmed to him. For the first ten minutes, they got along well together, but Keegan was always impatient. He didn't believe that a woman should be wooed. The dreary, slow business of breaking the ice, manoeuvring, spending money on a woman bored him. A girl either wanted it or she didn't. It was as simple as that.

Sheila was wearing a white bra and tight fitting red, cotton slacks. It was while she was leaning over the bar to help herself to another olive that Keegan pulled back the elastic of her slacks and slid down his hand, his fingers closing around her bare buttocks.

For a brief moment, Sheila remained motionless. Her flesh crawled with horror as she felt the smooth, soft fingers outraging her privacy. Then she swung around, jerking his hand away and slammed her handbag against his face. The metal clasp of the handbag struck his nose. As he reeled back, his face suddenly a mask of blood, she ran frantically out of the bar.

The bartender, who had witnessed what had happened, offered a towel.

'A good try, Buster,' he said admiringly. 'You got more nerve than me. How did it feel?'

Keegan used the towel to mop up the blood, then he tossed the towel back to the bartender. He put three one dollar bills on the counter. His small, green eyes gleamed as he said, 'Thanks, Joe. You never know with women, do you?' and holding his handkerchief to his still bleeding nose, he left the bar.

Hitting Keegan was as dangerous as slapping at a black mamba. Sheila Latimer had no idea what she had started. She was furious, ashamed and revolted by what this man had done to her. She rushed back to her rented room and took a shower, vigorously scrubbing herself to get rid of the creepy feeling of the fingers that had touched her.

Out of the shower, suddenly lonely, not knowing what her future would be, sickened by this blond, baby-faced man's behaviour, she threw herself on the bed and wept.

Sheila had no one to turn to. She had quarrelled with her parents, small minded, disapproving people who lived on a Mid-West farm and from where Sheila had escaped to Miami where she worked as a hotel receptionist. Hoping for something more exciting than coping with half drunk, idiotic tourists, she had entered for the Beauty competition. She knew no one in Paradise City where the competition had been held. As a runner up, she had been promptly dropped. The fat, bored agent who had arranged everything for her immediately lost interest when she failed to win the competition. Now, she would have to return to Miami and hope to get her hotel job back.

She spent a miserable, restless night. Every so often she woke, still feeling in her imagination the groping soft fingers on her body. A little after seven o'clock, as she was turning uneasily in her bed, wondering if she shouldn't get up and make herself a cup of coffee, she heard the front doorbell ring. She sat up. It could be a telegram! There might be an offer from her agent!

Struggling into a wrap, she ran across the room and opened the door.

Chet Keegan pushed his way in. Before she could scream, his clenched fist struck her on the side of her jaw and she fell forward at his feet. He closed the door, dragged her to the bed and threw her on it.

He collected a brief-case he had brought with him. From it, he took four short lengths of cord. He tied her ankles and wrists to the bed. Then he took from the brief-case a hypodermic syringe and a rubber topped bottle.

It took five nightmare days and nights to turn Sheila Latimer into a craven, broken heroin addict. When Keegan was satisfied that she was broken, he left her, leaving her his telephone number, sure she would call him. Two days later, she was babbling over the telephone line, hysterically begging him to help her. He went to her apartment with the necessary fix. Before giving her the fix, he used and abused her. Whatever he demanded, whatever he did to her, meant nothing to her. The needle that sank into her vein was the overwhelming need in her life.

So now, she was Keegan's slave.

Two days after Nona Jacey's arrest, Sheila pulled up outside Mrs. Watson's apartment house. She got out of the Opel Kadett that Keegan had given her and walked up the steps to the front door.

She was feeling pretty good. Keegan had given her a fix an hour or so ago, and she was relaxed and more than willing to do what she had been told to do.

She rang the bell and waited. There was some delay, then the door opened. Mrs. Watson regarded her with disapproval and suspicion.

'What is it?' she demanded, hugging her grubby shawl to her.

'I am Sheila Mason,' Sheila said, repeating the dialogue Keegan had made her memorize. 'I am Nona Jacey's cousin. As you know, Nona is in trouble. She won't be coming back. I am here to pay her rent and to take her things.'

'That little thief!' Mrs. Watson's face turned sour. 'To think of it! Shop-lifting! Well, she deserves what she got! You don't take her things until the rent has been paid . . . she owes me a month. That'll be a hundred dollars!'

Pay her what she asks, Keegan had said. She is certain to rob you, but pay her.

Sheila opened her bag and took the money Keegan had given her from it. She gave Mrs. Watson two fifty dollar bills. 'May I have the key, please? I want to pack her things.'

Mrs. Watson studied the two bills, then nodded. She stared at the blonde, white-faced girl curiously.

'I didn't know she had a cousin,' she said. 'She never mentioned you.'

'I'm from Texas,' Sheila said, following Keegan's dialogue. 'She will be returning with me when she is released.'

Mrs. Watson snorted.

'I wouldn't have her back here,' she said. 'Take her things and let me have the room.' She slammed the door.

Sheila mounted the stairs. Chet, she thought, would be pleased. It was really very simple. If he was really pleased, he might leave her alone tonight and he might give her a stronger fix.

She felt almost light-hearted as she unlocked the door on the third floor and entered Nona's deserted apartment.

Lindsey decided he would have to handle personally the next phase of the operation. Neither Silk nor Keegan had the know-how to cope successfully with Dr. Alex Kuntz.

He dialled the doctor's number and after three attempts, finally got past the busy signal. A woman's voice, cool and impersonal answered.

'I would like an appointment with Dr. Kuntz,' Lindsey said. 'Either this afternoon or tomorrow morning.'

'I am sorry . . . Dr. Kuntz has no free time until the end of next week. Could I suggest Friday week at three?'

Expecting such an answer, Lindsey said, 'No, I'm also sorry. Please consider this as an emergency. It must be this afternoon or at the latest tomorrow morning.'

'Who did you say was calling?' Her voice now was cautious.

'This is Jonathan Lindsey. Would you be kind enough to tell Dr. Kuntz that I am acting on behalf of Mr. Herman Radnitz? I believe he knows him.'

There was a pause, then the woman said, 'Please hold on.'

Lindsey reached for a boiled sweet from a jar he kept on the desk. Although he didn't smoke or drink, he was an addict to sucking boiled sweets. There was a long delay, then the woman said, 'Dr. Kuntz will see you this evening at six o'clock.'

Lindsey smiled to himself.

'Thank you . . . I'll be there,' and he hung up.

Two minutes after six o'clock, Lindsey left his Cadillac Fleetwood, parked outside Dr. Kuntz's impressive mansion that overlooked the yacht harbour in Greater Miami, and walked up the seven marble steps. He rang the doorbell.

A nurse came to the door: a faded, elderly experienced looking woman who gave him a hard stare and a brief impersonal smile as she led him into a big, ornately furnished waiting-room.

'Dr. Kuntz will not keep you for more than a few minutes,' she said and Lindsey recognized the voice he had heard over the telephone.

He nodded and sat down, reaching for the latest copy of *Life*. Four minutes later, the door swung open and the nurse said, 'Dr. Kuntz will see you now.'

Lindsey followed her down a passage and paused with her outside an oak panelled door. She knocked softly, then opened the door and stood aside.

Lindsey walked into a room where a fat, short man, wearing a short sleeved double breasted white overall sat at a desk. To his right was a leather covered couch. Cabinets containing various surgical instruments lined the walls.

'Nice of you to see me at such short notice,' Lindsey said, his charming smile in evidence. He took the chair facing Dr. Kuntz and sat down.

Dr. Kuntz regarded him, his fat face expressionless. His bald head, his black bushy eyebrows, his small hooked nose and thin lips made up a picture of cold, efficient professionalism. A patient, facing him, would draw confidence from such a face: a man who knew his business and who would be impatient and ruthless with hypochondriacs.

The two men regarded each other. Lindsey, relaxed, was in no hurry to begin. He had decided that Kuntz should make the first approach. Finally, Kuntz said cautiously, 'You come from Mr. Radnitz?'

'That's right. I work for him.' Lindsey crossed one long leg over the other and regarded the glossy toe-cap of his Lobb handmade shoe, then he looked straight into Kuntz's eyes. 'You probably remember him?'

Kuntz picked up a gold fountain pen and turned it between his fat fingers.

'I think the name is familiar,' he said finally.

Lindsey laughed. He had an easy, infectious laugh, quiet, almost a chuckle, that usually set other people laughing. Dr. Kuntz remained poker-faced, his fingers turning the pen.

Again there was a long pause, then Lindsey decided he was wasting time. He came abruptly to the point.

'I have a patient for you, doctor,' he said. 'It will be necessary for you to close your office and give up three or four weeks of your time while you look after this patient. He is a V.I.P. You will be paid a fee of ten thousand dollars. You will be needed in six days' time . . . the third.'

Kuntz put down the gold fountain pen. His bushy eyebrows climbed to the top of his head.

'That is quite impossible,' he said. 'I will be happy to treat your patient, but he must come here. I am far too busy to leave my office for such a length of time.'

'But have you an alternative, doctor?' Lindsey asked smiling. 'Perhaps I can bore you with a little story? In 1943, a certain brilliant brain specialist was living in Berlin. He volunteered—not under any pressure—to work in a certain concentration camp, so that he could experiment on Jewish prisoners. It is on record that this man murdered two thousand three hundred and twenty-two Jews before he perfected a certain brain operation. This operation was of considerable advantage to people suffering from manic depression. It is now recognized by medical science as a major breakthrough. This doctor, whose name was Hans Schultz, made other and less important experiments. Again it is on record that he murdered some five hundred Jews without achieving anything very important. I have documentary proof of this. I have also photographs of this doctor actually at work. These photographs and the documents have been given me by Mr. Radnitz who you may remember was also active during the Nazi régime. But this is neither here nor there. It so happens we need your skill. We have a V.I.P. patient. The fee is ten thousand dollars, and of course, silence. Dr. Hans Schultz is believed dead. He can remain dead, provided you are willing to co-operate.'

The small, fat man again reached for his gold fountain pen. Again he turned it between his fingers, then he looked up and regarded Lindsey with stone cold, expressionless eyes.

'Very interesting,' he said quietly. 'The third did you say? Yes, then perhaps I could arrange to be free for—you said three weeks? Yes, I suppose that is possible.' The black, beady eyes moved over Lindsey's relaxed face. 'And who is the patient?'

'We will go into that on the third.'

'I understand.' The fat fingers moved to a bell push on the desk and hovered over it. 'Then what are the arrangements?'

'I will be here at ten o'clock on the morning of the third. We will drive together to a certain place and you will stay there, looking after the patient for a period of three or four weeks. You will bring everything you need. Any additional things I can collect for you.'

Kuntz nodded, then thumbed down the bell push.

'You did say ten thousand dollars?' he said, peering with greed in his small black eyes.

'Yes. You will receive your fee when your work has proved satisfactory.'

The faded, elderly nurse came into the room and Lindsey got to his feet.

'See you on the third, doctor,' he said, and nodding, he followed the nurse to the front door.

He walked to the Cadillac, humming softly under his breath. As he got under the driving wheel, he opened the glove compartment and helped himself to a boiled sweet from a number he kept there in a glass jar.

Acting on instructions and information supplied by Lindsey, Chet Keegan pulled up outside the Go-Go Club, a brash nitery that catered mainly for the nautical trade. Sailors, coming off visiting warships, needed lots of hard liquor, lots of willing girls and lots of strident music. The Go-Go Club provided all this. Since it skimmed off the rowdies, the toughies and the troublemakers and knew how to handle them, the police were content to live and let live. It was seldom that they were called in to quell a disturbance. The Go-Go Club bouncers were professionals and could stop a fight before it got started. There were six of them.

What they didn't know about dirty fighting, the use of a cosh and the stunning blow from a fist wrapped in brass wasn't worth knowing. There were times when some foolhardy sailors, lit up with whisky, would start trouble just for the hell of it, but the trouble was invariably cut short and the sailors invariably laid out in the parking lot to recover from a vicious beating from these six professionals. Having recovered, they would return to their ships, nursing their wounds, wiser and more prudent men.

The girls working at the Club were handpicked. They were all under the age of twenty-four. A number of them were prostitutes, the rest, girls in search of excitement. All of them were capable of handling any man. They wore as a uniform a skimpy bra and silk panties, high-heeled gold shoes and a carnation fixed over their navels with surgical tape. Across the seat of their panties were printed various slogans: *Don't Park Here. This Belongs To Me. No Place For Hands. Cul-de-Sac. No Entry,* and so on.

The Belle of the twenty girls at the Club was Drena French. According to the information Lindsey had received from his Detective Agency, this girl had arrived in Paradise City some eighteen months ago. She was twenty-two years of age, with raven black hair, sensually beautiful, with the morals of an alley cat and a lump of quartz where her heart should have been.

It was this girl that Keegan, on Lindsey's instructions, wished to see. He entered the Club, nodded to the doorman who gave him an oily smile, handed his hat to the hat check girl who gushed over him, then, pushing aside the red velvet curtain that screened the entrance, walked into the noisy, smoke ladened room that made up the Club. There were some thirty odd sailors already having themselves a ball, and a few well dressed men, probably Advertising Account Executives, trying to find relaxation, and, of course, the girls.

Keegan spotted Shane O'Brien who ran the Club. He worked his way around the tightly packed tables, shook his head at the three girls who were advancing hopefully towards him and came to rest at O'Brien's side.

O'Brien was a tall, rangy Irishman with a broken nose, red hair and steel blue eyes.

As Keegan came out of the smoke ladened atmosphere, O'Brien looked warily at him. He didn't like Keegan. He knew he was dangerous and a professional killer.

'Hi, Shane,' Keegan said. 'Looks like you have a big house.'

'It's early yet,' O'Brien returned. 'It'll be quite a night by two o'clock. There's a Flat-top parked in the bay. The boys keep coming.'

'Yeah.' Keegan lit a cigarette. 'Where's Drena?'

O'Brien looked away.

'She's busy. What's she to you?'

Keegan smiled at him. His small green eyes glittered viciously.

'Look, Mick, relax. I want her. I've business with her. So suppose you go get her?'

O'Brien eyed him. Big as he was, plus his six bouncers, he was still scared of Keegan.

'Now look, friend, she is valuable to me. She does a good job here. I don't want her doing business with you.'

'No?' Keegan continued to smile. 'Well, that's too bad. Run along, Mick, and get her. I could come in some other night with

Lu. He and I could have a ball. Lift the feet, Irish. I want her.'

O'Brien recognized a threat when he heard it. He hesitated, then decided Drena wasn't worth his Club being smashed up. He moved away. Keegan sat at one of the empty tables. A waiter came swiftly to his side. Keegan shook his head at him and the waiter went away.

Drena French pushed her way through a group of sailors, protecting her behind with her hands. She was wearing the Club uniform. The slogan printed across her neat hips read: *Fanny Is My Name—Frantic Is My Nature.*

She paused beside Keegan, regarding him. She thought he was quite a doll, but she was alert and suspicious. O'Brien had warned her this man was dangerous.

'What is it, honey?' she asked, leaning over him.

'Get changed,' Keegan said, 'and meet me outside in ten minutes. I've a proposition for you.'

Drena laughed.

'Come on sweetheart, be your age. I work here. I can't quit at this hour. Besides, I'm not interested in propositions. That's terribly old hat.'

Keegan managed to control the urge to slap her pretty face. Even he didn't want to tangle with O'Brien's six bouncers. Containing his vicious temper, he said, 'But you will be interested, baby. It's big money. I have a little job lined up for you. The pay-off is in five beautiful, fat figures.'

Drena stiffened, staring at him.

'You kidding?'

'No.' Keegan took out his wallet and produced three one hundred dollar bills. He let her see them, then folded them, and getting to his feet, he tucked them into her bra. 'Hurry it up, baby. In ten minutes,' and he walked out of the Club.

O'Brien came through the cigarette smoke and dim lights.

'What gives?' he demanded.

'I don't know.' Drena took the three folded bills from her bra and showed them to him. 'He says he wants me to do a job.' She was about to tell O'Brien that Keegan had talked of five figures, but decided that she could be talking too much. 'Can I run along, Shane?'

'I can't stop you,' O'Brien said. 'But watch it. This guy is as cute as a cobra and as loving as a dose of poison.'

'Well, it can't kill me to hear what he wants,' Drena said. 'I can take care of myself,' then turning, she walked away, swishing her hips. the lettering on her panties jerking.

Fifteen minutes later, wearing a shabby nylon dress and down-at-the-heel shoes, she walked out of the Club.

Keegan was sitting in the Thunderbird. He swung open the car door and she slid in beside him.

'That big Mick doesn't like you,' she said, leaning back, adoring the luxury of the car. 'He says you are poison.'

'Yeah?' Keegan started the car and drove into the steady flow of traffic. 'Maybe I am.'

He drove to a deserted part of the beach, stopped the car and turned off the lights.

'Okay, baby, let's talk business,' he said. 'First, the pay-off. Play the cards I deal you right and you will pick up ten thousand dollars. Just in case you have wax in your ears and think I'm kidding, the pay-off is ten thousand dollars—repeat ten thousand dollars.'

Drena gaped at him. She looked into the small, cold, green eyes and a wave of excitement crawled up her long, beautifully formed spine. This man meant what he said. Years of experience, dealing with men, told her this.

'Keep talking,' she said, her voice shaking, her hands into fists. 'This makes beautiful music.'

'Doesn't it?' Keegan said. 'Ten thousand dollars could buy you a ball.' He lit a cigarette without offering her one. Keegan had no polish. To him, women were to be used and abused and certainly not to be considered. 'Your little pal, Fred Lewis. I'm interested in him.'

Drena started and stared at him in surprise.

'Freddy? But why?'

'Look, baby, I do the talking. You answer the questions. Lewis . . . how are you two getting along together?'

She shrugged, grimacing.

'Well, he's a drip. Maybe later . . . I don't know. He wants to marry me. One day, perhaps, when I've had enough of the Club, I'll decide, but not now.'

'How does he feel about it?'

Drena shrugged impatiently.

'He's crazy about me.' She shook her head. 'Okay, I admit it's nice for a girl who works the way I work to have some poor sap just mad about her. But he hasn't any money. A girl can't get along without money.'

'Has he ever laid you?' Keegan asked.

Drena sat bolt upright. 'What the hell is that to do with you?' she demanded. 'I'll have you know . . .'

'Brake the yak,' Keegan said, not bothering to look at her, but staring through the windshield at the gently moving sea. 'I asked you . . . have you given him anything?'

Drena hesitated, then shrugged.

'If you have to know . . . when a sap wants to marry a girl that bad, she keeps her legs crossed. Do you imagine I am soft in the head?'

Keegan leaned over the back of his seat and brought up a brief-case lying on the rear seat. He laid it across his knees. Zipping it open, he turned on the dashboard light, then said, 'Feed your eyes on this, baby.'

Drena caught her breath. In the case, neatly arranged were packets of $50 bills . . . more money than she had ever seen in her life.

'That's what ten thousand dollars looks like,' Keegan said. 'All yours if you can handle this deal.'

He let Drena stare at the bills for several seconds, then he zipped the case shut.

'Tell me,' she said, her breathing fast. 'Short of murder, I'm right with you, you gorgeous, beautiful man.'

Keegan told her.

The Harrison Wentworth Sanatorium is situated on the far left arm of Paradise Bay with views over the sea and the distant yacht harbour: a massive building standing in some three acres of immaculately kept lawns. It is surrounded by high walls and there is a lodge at the entrance gates where an elderly guard checks in visitors with old-world charm.

The security regulations are strict. Each patient is double locked in his room and each corridor is watched over by a qualified male nurse. The rooms are air conditioned, the windows of armoured glass and they don't open. There is no hint that this mansion is a prison, and it is on record that no patient has ever escaped once consigned to a room.

The Sanatorium is the most expensive and most exclusive criminal asylum for the insane in the world. It provides accommodation for two hundred patients, and at this period there were one hundred and twenty-two patients: all people of importance, some young, most of them old, at least fifty of them highly dangerous but all with wealth.

Apart from Dr. Max Hertz who owned the asylum, two resident doctors and a Matron, the staff consisted of ten male nurses. Each one of these male nurses had been secretly investigated by Lindsey's Detective Agency. From their reports, Lindsey had finally decided that Fred Lewis was the most likely of them all to work on.

Lindsey discovered from the report that Lewis was young, besotted by a dance hostess, urgently in need of money and dissatisfied with his work.

Lindsey knew the approach would have to be made through this dance hostess. He was sure she could handle Lewis and persuade him to co-operate so long as she was satisfied her reward would be impressive. That was why he had given Keegan $10,000 in cash with which to dazzle her. With that incentive, a woman of her record could achieve a miracle.

Fred Lewis, a small, slimly built young man in his late twenties, with a crewcut of black hair, a sun-tanned, rather chubby face, signed off duty at eight p.m.

Dr. Max Hertz, a big, balding man with a genial fleshy face, leaned back in his desk chair to ask, 'All under control up there, Fred? No trouble?'

'No, sir. Mr. Massingham is a little restless. I told Jack. He is giving him a sedative. The rest of them are behaving beautifully.' He signed off, replacing the pen in Hertz's pen rack.

'Then see you tomorrow,' Hertz said.

'Yes, sir. Good night, sir.'

Lewis left the mansion and walked around to the car park. He got into his shabby, second-hand Buick. He drove down to the gates. The guard, Harry Edwards, came out of the lodge to open up. Edwards was a rotund man in his late sixties. He had been gate-man now for the past thirty years.

'Hi, Fred,' he said, unlocking the gates. 'How's that little doll you're chasing?'

Fred forced a grin.

'I'll tell you tomorrow.'

'Don't do anything I shouldn't hear about,' Edwards said. He envied Lewis his youth. 'But if you do, confide in me.'

Again Fred forced a grin, then drove out on to the beach road that curved around the Bay and led to the centre of the City.

His grin quickly faded once he was out of sight of Edwards. He now regretted boasting to Edwards about his association with Drena French. But he had had to confide in someone. At least, Edwards didn't kid him as Lewis knew the rest of the staff would have kidded him. He had known Drena French now for three months. One night, suddenly sick of his tiny airless apartment, he had wandered into the Go-Go Club. It had been an off-night. No warships were in the bay and Drena was glad to have a dancing partner. She found this rather serious, decent young man an enormous change from her usual brash, pawing nautical clients. He held her as if she was a precious piece of china. She could see the look of bewildered worship growing in his eyes as the evening moved along. This was something that hadn't ever happened to her. Slightly intrigued, she had impulsively invited him back to her room when the Club shut down. She imagined it would be an experience to have such a man in her bed. But Fred Lewis didn't attempt to make love to her. He sat on the edge of a chair and talked and adored her with his eyes. He drank one small whisky, then around three o'clock in the morning, he got to his feet and said it was time for him to go home. Drena very nearly spoilt the atmosphere he had created by inviting him to share her bed. Something warned her not to do so, and she saw him to the door. He kissed her hand and this completely threw her. No man had ever done that before. Usually they slapped her behind and tried to get their hands down the front of her bra.

From then on, Lewis was continually at the Club during his nights off: dancing with her, spending more money than he could afford, and dreaming about her.

Later, some two months after they had first met, he proposed.

'Look, Drena, we could get married,' he said, his hands squeezing his knees, his face anxious and tense. 'I don't earn a lot, but we could manage. I love you. I want to get you out of this Club. What do you say?'

Drena had never had a proposal of marriage before. She was a little emotional about it, but not for long. Lewis had become a habit. She liked his adoration, but the idea of living with him in a poky, airless apartment, doing the shopping, preparing his meals was just one hell of a joke.

'I'm not ready yet to get married, Fred,' she had returned. 'Maybe later, but not yet.'

Lewis accepted this. At least she hadn't turned him down. But as the weeks passed, his longing for her increased. He would have to leave his job, he kept telling himself. He would have to find something that paid better. But what? This depressed him. He knew his nursing training fitted him for nothing else. Maybe, if he studied at night, he might become a doctor. He discussed this with Drena who was slightly intrigued. She said she wouldn't mind being married to a doctor, but she pointed out he couldn't expect to do his work at the Sanatorium and work nights. When would she ever see him?'

Lewis was thinking about this as he parked his car before the dreary brown-stone building where he lived. He walked up the three flights of stairs and let himself into his small, drab apartment. He turned on the light and then went into the kitchenette and looked into the refrigerator. There was some cold spaghetti and a slice of rather dry ham he had put aside for his supper. It was while he was eating this that the telephone bell rang. Surprised, he answered.

'Freddy? Drena.' He felt a rush of blood up his spine at the sound of her voice. 'I want to talk to you. I'm on my way.'

'Now?' Lewis was startled. 'It's after nine! Don't you have to be at the Club?'

'In a pig's ear!' Drena said. 'I'm on my way,' and she hung up.

Bewildered and excited, Lewis wolfed down the remains of his supper, then wondering if Drena had eaten, he checked his savings and found a $20 bill tucked away in one of his drawers. He sighed with relief. If she wanted to be taken out, he had the money.

But Drena didn't want to be taken out. She arrived looking overwhelming in a tight fitting blue shirt and a mini-skirt. She brought with her a bottle of Scotch and a big packet of Club sandwiches.

As soon as they were settled on the divan, eating the sandwiches, she said, 'We could get married, Freddy, or have you changed your mind?'

Lewis gaped at her, his eyes unbelieving, his half eaten sandwich hovering before his mouth. Then he put down the sandwich and turned to face her.

'Changed my mind? Drena! How could you even suggest such a thing! I don't understand.'

'We could be married as soon as you can get the licence,' Drena said calmly. 'Next week . . . something's come up.'

Lewis timidly touched her hand.

'You're not kidding? You really mean we—we could get married next week?'

'That's what the girl said.'

'Oh, God! Yes! But I don't understand. What do you mean . . . something's come up?'

'There's a crummy seafood restaurant right opposite Watson's jetty. In case you don't know, the jetty is always used by the sailors coming off their ships, anchored in the bay. The restaurant is owned by Jeff Hawkins—an old buddy of mine. The trouble with him is he has a sour-puss wife so his waitresses are old, fat and gruesome. He doesn't get the sailor trade.' Drena paused to take a bite at her sandwich, then went on, her mouth full. 'He wants out. If you and I bought this restaurant we could turn it into a gold mine. The cook would stay on and he knows his stuff. We could get three of the girls from the Club as waitresses and with me behind the cash desk and you running the place, we would be a riot. Moe Linsky who is the best and toughest bouncer at the Go-Go would join us to keep order. Freddy! We really are on to something!' She put her hand on his, her eyes sparkling. 'We can't go wrong. There's accommodation above the restaurant . . . a bedroom, a decent sitting-room. The whole place would have to be given a lick of paint, but that wouldn't cost much. I would want a juke-box. How do you like the idea?'

Lewis regarded her blankly.

'But where's the money coming from? How much does this friend of yours want for the restaurant?'

'I've already talked to him. He'll take seven thousand dollars spot cash,' Drena said. 'It's a knock down price. Don't think I didn't have to haggle . . . God! How I haggled! We can get it for seven thousand! Think of it! You and me married! Owning a restaurant that can't go wrong! In a few years we could open another restaurant. In another few years we will have a Cadillac and me a mink coat!'

Lewis said quietly, 'Look, Drena, what's the matter with you tonight?' Or are we playing a game of let's pretend?'

'Pretend? Nothing! We can swing this, Freddy!'

'Can we? Where's the seven thousand coming from?'

She laughed.

'Ah . . . that's the big question. It's coming from you.'

Lewis moved uneasily.

'But you know, Drena, I haven't that kind of money.'

'You will have. I met a guy last night who is ready to pay you ten thousand dollars,' Drena said, smiling at him. 'Ten thousand gorgeous, beautiful dollars in cash! We buy the restaurant for seven and we have three to spend on the place. After that, we are in business. What do you say?'

Lewis stared. He was wondering if she were drunk or had gone crazy.

'Who is he? Drena! What are you saying?'

Drena knew she was approaching the tricky part of this proposition. She had laid the bait, but now the fish had to rise.

'This is a chance in a lifetime, Freddy,' she said, her fingers stroking his hand. 'This guy will pay us all that money if you will co-operate. All I'm asking you to do is to co-operate. If you do, we get married next week, we buy the restaurant and we're set. For this money, this guy wants a patient out of the asylum. You can tell him how to do it. That's all there is to it. Do that, and we get the money.'

Lewis sat motionless, his eyes suddenly scared.

'I don't understand,' he said finally. 'A patient out of the asylum? Drena! What are you talking about?'

'Would it be so difficult to get a patient out?' she asked. 'I shouldn't have thought so. If you can't do it, we don't get the restaurant and we don't get married. I'll have to stay at the Club, getting pawed every night, growing older until I get thrown out. And then what will I do? I'm telling you right now, Freddy, if you don't co-operate, you will lose me. I can't live on your level. I'm sorry, but that's the way it is. We now have a chance of a real breakthrough. If you won't take it, then it's goodbye.'

Lewis studied her, then realized she meant just what she said.

'I'm not losing you, Drena,' he said quietly. 'That's for real. Life without you would mean nothing to me. All right, what do I have to do?'

Drena drew in a long, slow breath. She had been fairly sure of success, but she hadn't imagined it would be this easy.

CHAPTER THREE

THE WOMEN' HOUSE OF CORRECTION, Paradise City, is reached by a two-mile long, lonely road that branches off State Highway 4A to Greater Miami.

At eight o'clock on a bright sunny morning, the gates opened and five girls came out into the hot sunshine. One of them was Nona Jacey. The other four were about her age, and they had completed much longer sentences. They regarded Nona as the baby of the family. All of them considered it rough luck that she had been picked up at the Self-Service store. They had been kind to her during her week's stay behind bars, kidding her along, advising her next time to watch out for the store's dick.

Still stunned, still scarcely believing this had happened to her, Nona had listened to their chatter, knowing it would be useless to try to convince these girls that she hadn't stolen anything, and for reasons she just couldn't understand, she had been framed.

There was a shabby, dusty bus waiting to take the girls to the centre of the City. Also parked nearby was a Buick car. As the girls moved towards the bus, two men slid out of the Buick and came towards them.

Lu-Lu Dodge, a hardbitten blonde who had served a three-year stretch for sticking a knife into her pimp, studied the two men as they approached.

She said, 'Ah-ha . . . cops! Now who's in trouble?'

The two men converged on the group of girls, and to Nona's alarm, came to rest before her.

'Nona Jacey?' one of the men said. He towered above her like a mountain of granite.

'Yes.'

The other girls hurried towards the bus, but Lu-Lu stayed, glaring at the two men.

The man flashed a badge.

'Police. You're wanted at headquarters. We have a car. Come on.'

'Hey!' Lu-Lu exclaimed, pushing her way between the two men and Nona. 'Dig a lake, copper, then jump into it.' She put her hand on Nona's arm. 'You stick right with me, honey. If these creeps have business with you, they can do it in the City.'

The second man, bulky, with a red, freckled face, moved forward. His shoulder slammed against Lu-Lu, sending her reeling, then he shoved her towards the bus.

'On your way, Cheapie,' he snarled. 'Don't think we can't put you under the wraps for years.'

The other man was leading Nona towards the Buick.

Terrified, she was saying, 'I don't understand. What is it? Why am I wanted?'

'Look, sister, if anyone told me anything, I would be happy,' the man at her side said in a bored flat voice. 'But no one ever does. They want you. I'm told to pick you up . . . so I pick you up.'

They reached the car and Nona got into the front seat. She looked back at Lu-Lu who was watching. Lu-Lu waved to her. The other man joined them, got in the back seat, and the Buick went fast down the dusty road.

Once out of sight of the prison and away from the following bus, the man, sitting at the back, leaned forward and his big, sweaty hands closed around Nona's throat. Powerful fingers dug cruelly into her windpipe. She reared back, but she was helpless in his grip. For a long moment, her legs thrashed, making the driver swerve and curse, then as the grip tightened, she went limp. The man on the back seat, put his hands under her armpits and dragged her over the seat into the back of the car. Working quickly, while the car raced down the long, deserted road, he strapped her hands and ankles together with strips of adhesive tape. Then he forced a rolled up handkerchief into her mouth and strapped on yet another strip of tape to keep the handkerchief in place. He shoved her to the floor of the car, then threw a rug over her.

'Hurry it up, pal,' he said anxiously.

These two men, working for Lindsey's Detective Agency, were uneasy. They knew the penalty for kidnapping, but they were being well paid. Their one thought was to finish the job quickly.

A mile or so before the branch road met the highway, the black Thunderbird was waiting. The Buick skidded to a stop and the two men bundled Nona's unconscious body from the back of their car to the floor of the Thunderbird.

'Any trouble?' Silk asked, the sunlight reflecting on his glass eye.

'No.'

'Then get lost, pronto.' Silk nodded to Keegan who sent the Thunderbird racing to the highway.

Half an hour later, the car began to climb into the foothills that lay some thirty miles behind Paradise City. Satisfied there was no car following, Silk said, 'I'd better take a look at her. We don't want her to croak.'

'You can say that again.' Keegan pulled up.

Silk got out of the car and got into the back seat. He dragged Nona's unconscious body up on to the seat and took out the gag. Keegan watched.

'Pretty nice,' he said, his eyes running over the girl's limp body. 'That's a frame I could dig for.'

'Show me any woman's frame you can't dig for,' Silk said with contempt. 'Get moving!'

Grinning, Keegan set the car in motion. In a cloud of dust, they continued on into the foothills.

Silk lit a cigarette. Women meant nothing to him. When he was seventeen years of age, he had married a tramp, four years older than himself. He had discovered with dismay that with her, he was impotent. The marriage had broken up after two weeks. Disillusioned, still seeking an outlet for his frustrated sexual desires, he had gone with a number of prostitutes, a sordid, expensive and unsatisfactory experience. This kind of life went on for some years, then in a sudden frenzy of frustration, he had strangled one of the girls he had gone with. Since then, he had put women out of his mind. But he had discovered an immense satisfaction in his first killing. From time to time over the years while working as a Number's collector, he would find a girl, use her and kill her. Then he heard through the underworld that Lindsey was looking for a professional killer. The two men had met: terms had been arranged. There was a man Lindsey had been instructed to silence. Lindsey gave Silk his first assignment with him.

The victim was to be a C.I.A. Agent who had collected enough evidence to put Herman Radnitz behind bars for the rest of his life. This man had been working on his own without consulting his superiors. He wanted all the credit, and Lindsey, learning of this, knew the Agent had to be immediately silenced.

Very sure of himself, Silk underrated the assignment. He imagined all he had to do was to go to this man's apartment, ring on the front doorbell and shoot him with a silenced gun as he opened the door.

But it didn't work out that way. He went to the apartment and rang the bell, but the door was opened by the Agent's wife. This threw Silk off his stride. He entered the lobby and the Agent, waiting behind the door, screwed the barrel of his gun against the back of Silk's neck. Silk dropped his gun. The Agent had walked him into the sitting-room and had lined him up against the wall and told his wife to call the police.

With the cold, reckless courage that was to stand him in good stead in future years, Silk threw himself at the Agent, a stabbing knife in his hand. As he drove the knife into the Agent's chest, he was blinded by the gun flash. The bullet smashed against his cheekbone, tearing out his left eye. Bleeding, half stunned and half blind, Silk managed to knife the woman who was desperately trying to telephone the police. Somehow, he got out of the apartment, somehow, he got into his car. This was something he never talked about nor wanted to remember.

Later, after he had recovered from his wound, he became Lindsey's head assassin.

But Lindsey knew Silk couldn't operate efficiently on his own. It was expecting too much. He had to be provided with an assistant. Lindsey looked around and discovered Chet Keegan. This young man had no police record. He seemed to Lindsey to be promising material.

Lindsey had run into Keegan in a cellar club in New York. At that time, Keegan was a pimp, living on the earnings of several Call-girls. Lindsey had enough knowledge of human viciousness to know that Keegan would do anything for money. He arranged a meeting between Silk and Keegan, and then had listened to Silk's report.

'Yeah . . . this boy is good,' Silk had said. 'I can train him. Give him to me. He's what we're looking for.'

Silk and Keegan made an ideal combination. Both of them had good appearances. They always dressed well. They could mix in any strata of society. Neither of them had any human feelings. Both of them were greedy for money. There was nothing they wouldn't do so long as their bank balances increased. The only difference between the two men was their sexual outlook. Silk was now completely indifferent to women. Keegan lived for women. Silk accepted this fact although it bored him. What Keegan did in his spare time was no business of his, but when on the job, he made it plain to Keegan that he must lay off women. Vicious as he was, Keegan accepted the fact that Silk was his boss. Silk was a dedicated killer who got a kick out of killing and was one hundred per cent dangerous.

Another half hour's fast drive brought them to a high hill, surrounded by desert. At the foot of the hill was an opening to a tunnel that led to a series of caves. This was the hideout Lindsey had chosen and had equipped.

Keegan drove the Thunderbird down the long tunnel, his headlights picking out the way, then the car slid to a stop as it entered the first big cave.

Three men, wearing jeans and sweat shirts, came up to the car. Silk and Keegan got out.

'There she is, Jim,' Silk said to a big, heavily built man with a hard, fleshy face. 'Take her to her quarters.'

'I'll do it,' Keegan said. 'It'll be a pleasure.'

'Take her,' Silk said to the big man, ignoring Keegan, 'and listen. Keep your hands off her. If I catch you mauling her, I'll kill you . . . understand?'

'Okay, Mr. Silk,' Jim said. 'She's my mother.'

He reached into the car and picked Nona off the back seat. Carrying her carefully, he walked away into the darkness.

Keegan watched, then sneered.

'What you want, Lu, is a shot of hormones. You should catch up with your living.'

The single, glittering eye regarded Keegan. The scarred face could have been carved out of stone.

'One of these days, little boy,' Silk said softly, 'you'll flap too much with your mouth.'

He walked away down the tunnel.

Keegan tried to grin, but it didn't come off. He hated to admit it, but Silk, even when he was in a friendly mood, made him uneasy. He began to take three suitcases from the Thunderbird. He tried to whistle, but found, to his irritation, his lips were dry.

The Crab and Lobster restaurant was a modest building that faced the oily waters of the commercial harbour where the sponge-diving boats tied up for the night. The restaurant had the advantage of four private rooms where one could eat decently, talk in private and come and go without being seen.

Soon after ten p.m., Lindsey parked his Cadillac on the water-front, then walked to the restaurant. The owner, a fat, cheerful Greek, showed him immediately to one of the private rooms. Lindsey ordered a lobster sandwich and a lime juice and soda. He walked on to the small, screened balcony and looked down at the activity going on below him. A sponge trawler was edging its way into the harbour. A number of fishermen were lounging against the bollards, talking. Several girls, wearing bikinis, were hopefully displaying their bodies in search of trade.

Lindsey had eaten his sandwich and was lighting a cigar when Silk and Keegan joined him. They came out on to the balcony and sat in basket chairs.

Lindsey asked in his quiet, cultured voice, 'Well? How is it building?'

'It moves,' Silk said. 'We have the girl . . . no trouble. Lewis will be here any minute. Chet collects Dr. Kuntz tomorrow.'

'I don't want the girl interfered with,' Lindsey said, staring down at the harbour. 'I am relying on you, Silk, to see she is left alone.'

'That's okay,' Silk said. 'I've told them.'

'I must have her co-operation,' Lindsey went on. 'The whole plan hangs on her.'

'Yeah . . . yeah,' Silk said impatiently. 'I've got the photo.'

There came a tap on the door. Silk slid to his feet, his hand inside his jacket, his fingers closing on the butt of his ·38 automatic. He went quickly to the door. Keegan was already on his feet, moving out of sight behind the doorway on to the terrace, gun in hand.

Lindsey, remaining where he was, watched these two killers with satisfaction. Their movements were so quick, so silent, so smooth that even he was impressed.

Fred Lewis came into the dimly lit room.

Their guns out of sight, Silk and Keegan brought the bewildered man out on to the terrace. Keegan went back and locked the door. Silk shoved a chair towards Lewis and told him to sit down.

It was dark out on the terrace. Lewis couldn't see Lindsey clearly. He just saw a tall, thin man in a basket chair, his hands folded in his lap, his face in the shadows. Near him stood another tall, thin man and this man scared him. He sensed a threat and when a third man joined them, more slightly built, but still menacing, his fear increased.

'Well, Lewis, you know my terms,' Lindsey said quietly. 'I am offering you ten thousand dollars and I want your help. Paul Forrester is one of your personal patients, I believe?'

The discussion between the four men lasted an hour. Finally, arrangements were made and Lewis, white-faced and unnerved, but determined, left. Lindsey got to his feet and stretched.

'There must be no loose ends to this operation,' he said, staring out to sea. 'As soon as Forrester is missing, there will be an intensive inquiry. That young man could crack. He is expendable . . . you understand?'

'Sure,' Silk said. 'How about his girl friend?'

Not turning, Lindsey said, 'She is another loose end. If she ran into an accident, I wouldn't check to find out what happened to the money we are paying her. I would have thought someone could use ten thousand dollars if she can't claim it.'

Silk and Keegan exchanged glances, then the two men left the terrace and went down the stairs to the Thunderbird.

Nona Jacey opened her eyes and stared around her. Her hand went to her aching throat, then she struggled up. She found herself on a camp bed in what seemed to be a small, shadowy cave. The dim light cast shadows on the sandy floor. Terrified, she started to her feet, then a girl said out of the shadows, 'Take it easy, baby. How do you feel?'

Nona peered at the girl who came forward. Sheila Latimer's beauty did much to help control Nona's jumping nerves.

'Where am I?' she said, speaking with difficulty. 'Who—who are you?'

'Sit down, honey,' Sheila said and came further into the light. 'I'm sorry about all this. I can imagine just how you are feeling. Take the weight off your feet. You're all right. Nothing bad is going to happen to you.'

Nona sat limply on the bed and Sheila joined her.

'Do you want a drink? Want anything—coffee? You've only to say,' Sheila went on. 'Gee! That creep certainly treated you rough. Your poor throat's all bruised and swollen.'

'Who are you? Where am I?' Nona demanded, staring at the blonde girl beside her.

'I'll give it to you straight, honey,' Sheila said. 'You've been kidnapped. I'm the sucker who has to look after you. Call me Sheila. You're quite safe. Nothing bad is going to happen to you. I'll be with you all the time. You don't have to be scared. You're in a cave—you can see that. You have a job to do. This is big time, honey. The guys who are handling this are tough. I've been around with one of them for some time . . . honey, is he tough! So long as you do what they want, you'll be fine. Try to get away, try to act tricky and you're heading for a terrible time. Please, honey, listen to me. I thought I could handle this creep, but I found out different. Don't make my mistake. Take a look . . .' She pulled up her skirt to show her thighs riddled with needle shots. 'I'm a junkie. I must have a daily fix. That's what they'll turn you into if you don't co-operate. There's nothing I wouldn't do now to get my regular fix. I don't want you to have to go through this, honey. He ties you to a bed and gives you the needle and after a while you are fixed. After that, you don't care.' She smiled brightly at Nona who was staring at her in horror. 'As I don't care.' She paused, then went on, 'Some time tomorrow, they are getting Paul Forrester out of the asylum. From what they tell me, you got along well with him when you worked for him. Your job is to persuade him to crack a code. I don't understand what all that's about, but it is Big Time. You two get together, you do your stuff, he cracks the code and then you'll be as free as the air. See? It's that simple. You have nothing to worry about, honey. Now, how about a nice cup of coffee?'

The Harrison Wentworth Sanatorium was in darkness. The gateman was in bed, blissfully snoring. The time was twenty minutes after two a.m.

Silk and Keegan left the Thunderbird parked against the high wall of the Sanatorium within twenty yards of the gate. Together they walked to the gate, paused and looked through the iron railings up the long dark drive that led to the mansion.

'Go ahead,' Silk said. 'Show me how clever you are.'

Keegan produced a flashlight and examined the heavy lock of the gate.

'Like stealing dimes from a baby,' he said. He leaned against the gate, inserted a bent piece of steel into the lock, fiddled, then pressed and the gate swung open. 'See? No hands . . . as simple as that.'

'Get yourself a decoration, little boy,' Silk said and started up the drive. Keegan followed him. Finally, they arrived at the imposing entrance to the mansion.

'Go ahead . . . have yourself a ball,' Silk said, waving to the door.

Keegan examined the lock, then shook his head in wonderment. 'A kid could handle this one . . . a kid with one arm.'

'Just open it and stop flapping with your mouth,' Silk said.

Keegan opened the door and they moved silently into the dimly lit lobby. Lewis had given them a sketch plan of the place. They knew exactly where to go. Moving like ghosts, they climbed the broad stairs to the first floor.

Lewis was waiting for them. He came forward, his face white, sweat beads on his forehead, his eyes restless.

'Hi,' Silk said softly. 'Okay?'

Lewis nodded.

'You gave him the pill?'

Again Lewis nodded. His mouth was so dry he was unable to speak.

'It worked?'

Lewis tried to moisten his lips.

'Yes . . . I've just looked at him. He's right out,' he said hoarsely.

'Okay, let's go get him.'

As Lewis led the way down the corridor, Keegan drew from his hip pocket a leather covered cosh. He held it in his hand, behind his back, out of sight.

Lewis paused before the door. With a shaking hand, he inserted a key, opened the door and stood aside.

Silk moved into a small room containing a bed, fitted cupboards and a toilet in an annexe. On the bed was a man.

'That him?' he asked.

'Yes,' Lewis said.

Silk regarded the sleeping man. He looked at Keegan who had come forward. 'Can you handle him?'

'Sure,' Keegan said. 'Nothing to it.'

Silk turned to Lewis.

'Where are his clothes?'

Lewis opened one of the closets.

'They are all here.'

Silk took a blue tropical suit off a hanger. He tossed a shirt, underwear, socks and shoes on to the bed. Rolling these into a bundle, he nodded to Lewis. 'Okay, we're set.'

It was at this moment that Keegan stole up behind Lewis and hit him with the cosh on the top of his head. He hit him with terrible violence. Lewis's head seemed to crack apart. Blood spleashed against the wall as he fell forward.

Watching, Silk said, 'You're sure?'

Keegan wiped the cosh on Lewis's white coat.

'You ask him . . . he'll tell you.'

He walked over to an upright chair, picked it up and examined it. Then with brute strength, he broke off one of the legs. Carrying the leg, he went over to Lewis's dead body, lifted the dead head and rubbed the end of the leg in the blood and brains of the smashed skull. He dropped the chair leg, then walked to the bed, stripped off the sheet. With Silk's help he got the sleeping man across his shoulders.

The two men moved silently down the stairs and into the hot, star studded night.

The Go-Go Club closed at 4 a.m. Most of the girls had already gone home with sailor clients, but Drena French still sat on a stool at the bar, a little drunk, but happy. This would be her last night in the club. In a way, she had regrets. She liked O'Brien and she got along well with most of the girls and the barman, a big Jamaican, named Tin-Tin Washington. He was a special favourite of hers.

He was polishing the last of the glasses. Most of the lights had been turned off. O'Brien was in the office checking over the cash. Only three half drunk sailors were still hanging on to the bar. Three of the girls were putting on their coats.

'Time you hit the hay, baby,' Tin-Tin said. 'It's past four.' He looked at the two remaining bouncers and jerked his thumb at the sailors. They nodded and converged on them.

'Well, Buddy-boy, I guess you're right,' Drena said, sliding off the stool. 'Me for the hay.' She finished her whisky and shoved the glass towards the Jamaican. 'You won't be seeing me in this dump from now on. I'll tell you a secret . . . I've bought a restaurant.'

The Jamaican smiled. His big white teeth glittered in the one remaining light over the bar.

'Like I've bought the White House . . . in a pig's ear,' he said. 'You go get some sleep, honey.'

Drena supported herself against the bar and laughed.

'Oh, boy! Did you but know! Anyway, this time next week, take time off from this dump and come to my place. The drinks and all the food you can eat will be on the house. The Seagull. Hear me? At the far end of the waterfront. Anything you want—for free! I know how to take care of my friends.'

'Yeah, I'm sure,' Tin-Tin said, still smiling. 'Okay . . . see you tomorrow.'

'Don't believe it? Ask Hawkins. A beautiful deal. Me and my boy friend are going to run it. We have girls, a cook and a bouncer. We're going to knock this stinking joint sideways,' Drena said. 'Oh, Man! What a set-up! You come . . . everything on the house for a pal like you.

She weaved her way from the bar and headed to the changing-room. One of the sailors grabbed hold of her and tried to drag her on to his lap. Before the bouncer could move, Drena had grabbed up an empty beer bottle and had slammed it down on the sailor's head.

'What a joint!' she shrilled. 'What a lousy, goddam joint!'

Ten minutes later, she left the club. The cool night air struck her forcibly after the thick, hot atmosphere of the club. She started down the waterfront, swinging her handbag, singing softly, not quite believing that by tomorrow she would be worth ten thousand dollars.

Silk, standing in the shadows, watched her leave the club, then he moved after her. He had left Keegan to take the sleeping Paul Forrester to the cave hideout.

No loose ends, Lindsey had said. There was one more end to tie up. He noticed that Drena staggered a little as she walked along. That told him she was drunk. It would be easy, he thought, and quickened his pace.

At this hour, the waterfront was dark and deserted. Drena heard quick footfalls coming up behind her. She paused and turned, expecting some sailor who had followed her from the club. She wasn't frightened. She was confident she could handle any drunken sailor. She saw the tall thin outline of a man, coming towards her. That was the last thing she was to see.

It happened so quickly, she had no time to protect herself. She was facing a professional killer. The man stooped and she felt her ankles gripped. Before she could release the scream in her throat, she felt herself flying into space, then her head smashed against the prow of a dinghy and her body splashed into the oily water of the harbour.

Silk paused long enough to make sure she didn't come to the surface, then he walked away, unseen, towards the lights of the City.

Sergeant Joe Beigler of the City Police was on night duty. The wall clock showed twenty minutes past four a.m. He sat at his desk, the inevitable carton of coffee at his elbow, the inevitable cigarette between his lips. He was a big, powerfully built man in his late thirties. His hard, fleshy face was freckled. He was wearing a short sleeved shirt and the collar was open: the black knotted tie, dragged down.

Across the room with its rows of empty desks, Detective 3rd Grade Max Jacoby shared the watch. He was young, tall, dark and enthusiastic. He was going through a mass of reports, humming contentedly.

'Would you lay off that buzzing noise?' Beigler said. 'You're not in Sinatra's class although you may think you are.'

Jacoby leaned back in his chair and grinned.

'Sheer jealousy, Sarg,' he said. 'You should hear me when I really cut loose.'

'Get on with the work,' Beigler growled. 'Have you finished with those reports?'

'A few left.' Jacoby looked at the wall clock, shaking his head. 'Man! Can I use my bed!'

The telephone bell rang. Beigler scooped up the receiver in a powerful, hairy hand. He listened to the agitated voice. Watching him curiously, Jacoby saw that Beigler's face had become tense and he pushed back his chair, knowing it must be an emergency.

Beigler said into the mouthpiece, 'Don't touch anything. We'll have men with you in a few minutes. Yes, okay. Just wait.' He hung up, grabbed another telephone receiver that connected him direct to Operations room. 'Jack? Get four men out to the Harrison Wentworth Sanatorium pronto. There's an emergency up there! They are to stand guard. Tell them not to touch a thing.' He slammed down the receiver, then snatched at another telephone. 'Charlie . . . call Hess. Get him up to the Harrison Wentworth Asylum. Alert Homicide. We need the full treatment up there.' He hung up, then looking across at Jacoby who was listening to all this, he said, 'One of the nuts has escaped. He's killed his male nurse. Get road block set up. You handle it.'

'Description?' Jacoby asked as he reached for the telephone on his desk.

'We haven't one right now. Get the road blocks set up. Tell

them to check all identities. The man's name is Paul Forrester. He won't have any means of identifying himself.'

'Forrester!' Jacoby stiffened. 'Judas! That's . . .'

'I know who it is! Get on with it!' Beigler again grabbed the telephone receiver. 'Charlie . . . you got Hess? Fine. Get me the Chief.'

Chief of Police Frank Terrell slept lightly. The first ring of the telephone bell by the side of the double bed brought him instantly awake. His wife, Carrie, sleeping at his side, moaned and came awake much more slowly. Already sitting on the side of the bed, Terrell, a big man with sandy hair that stood on end and with a jutting aggressive jaw was saying, 'Yes, Joe? What is it?'

'We have trouble at the Harrison Wentworth,' Beigler told him. 'Paul Forrester has killed his nurse and has escaped.'

'Paul Forrester?' Terrell's voice shot up.

'Yeah. I'm setting up road blocks. Hess is on his way out there. What else do you want me to do?'

'Send a car for me, Joe. I'll be right with you.'

He hung up and began to scramble into his clothes.

Carrie, a large, comfortable looking woman, had got into her dressing-gown and had left the bedroom. By the time Terrell was dressed, she had a cup of coffee waiting for him.

He smiled affectionately at her.

'Thanks, honey. I couldn't live without you.' He gulped down the coffee.

Then they heard a car pull up outside their modest bungalow.

'Is it serious?' Carrie asked, following her husband to the front door.

'Yes . . . don't expect me back tonight. I'll call you when I have time.' He gave her a quick kiss and then hurried down the short garden path to the waiting car.

During the fast drive to police headquarters, Terrell considered what he had to do. He walked briskly up the steps leading to the Detectives' room where he found Beigler still issuing orders on the telephone.

'Okay, Joe,' he said as Beigler hung up. 'You get up there. You're sure it is Paul Forrester?'

'Dr. Hertz said so . . . he must know.'

'Okay, get off. I'll be along later,' and Terrell took over Beigler's desk. As Beigler left the room, Terrell picked up the telephone receiver. 'Charlie, get me Roger Williams.' A minute later, a man's voice said sleepily, 'This is Williams . . . what the heck is it?'

'This is Captain Terrell. Paul Forrester has broken out and is on the run.'

Terrell heard a quick intake of breath. Then Williams who was the Federal Agent in Greater Miami, now suddenly very alert, said, 'What action have you taken?'

'Road blocks. My men are at the asylum now. We'll need help. This only broke half an hour ago. I'm getting every man we have out of bed, but we'll want more. The C.I.A. must be told . . . Washington too. Can I leave all that to you?'

'I'll handle it,' Williams said. 'Unless he steals a car, he can't get far.'

'We haven't a description of him. Will you get one on the wire? I'm going up to the asylum now. You can contact me there.'

'Okay,' Williams said and hung up.

Terrell turned to Jacoby.

'You stay here, Max. Handle all calls. Anything important get me on R/T.'

'Yes, sir,' Jacoby said and as Terrell left, he walked over to Beigler's desk and sat down.

He looked at the wall clock. The time was fifteen minutes after five a.m. He had a depressing feeling that his bed was miles out of reach.

Dr. Max Hertz was endeavouring to keep calm. He sat behind his desk, a cup of black coffee close at hand, a cigarette burning a little feverishly between his lips. He was wearing a sky blue dressing-gown over white and blue piped pyjamas. His thinning hair was ruffled. He was certainly not looking his best.

'This has never happened before,' he was saying to Terrell who sat opposite him. 'This is a great shock. My sanatorium is the best there is. I don't have to tell you that. We have only the most important people here as patients. I have been in charge now for more than fifteen years. Not one patient has ever escaped . . . or attempted to escape.'

Terrell shifted restlessly.

'Well, one has,' he said. 'We have to find him. Just how did he escape?'

Dr. Hertz sipped his coffee, then put down the cup.

'I can only assume Lewis was careless. I don't like to say this because he and all my staff have been hand picked and more than trustworthy, but this seems to be the only possible explanation. We have strict security rules. At night, there are always two male nurses on duty on each floor. One of them sleeps, the other has a desk at the head of the stairs where he can watch every door to our patients' rooms. If the patient rings, the rule is that the nurse on duty must alert the nurse sleeping before he goes to the patient's room. These unfortunate people we have here are mostly dangerous. I suspect Lewis failed to follow my rules. Forrester rang for him and instead of disturbing Mason, who works the night shift with Lewis, Lewis foolishly went to Forrester's room alone. When I say foolishly, perhaps that is being harsh, for Forrester has shown no signs of violence. He has been the ideal patient, so, I suppose, Lewis felt justified in not disturbing Mason. I suppose when Lewis entered the room, he was attacked. Forrester then got the master key from Lewis, opened the front door and the door of the outside gate.'

Beigler put his head around the door. 'Excuse me, Chief . . .'

Terrell got to his feet.

'Okay, doctor, you can leave all this to us. There's just one thing . . . please don't talk to the press. Washington is coming into the picture and this could be a Top Secret thing.'

'Yes . . . yes, of course. I understand.'

Leaving the doctor sipping his coffee and trying to steady his shaking hands, Terrell joined Beigler in the corridor.

'Doc is doing a Sherlock Holmes act,' Beigler said, a resigned note in his voice. 'You'd better talk to him.'

Terrell followed Beigler up the stairs. They entered Paul Forrester's room where Detective Fred Hess of the Homicide Squad was sitting on the bed, writing in his notebook and Dr. Lowis, the M.O., was watching two ambulance attendants get Fred Lewis's body on to a stretcher.

Lowis, a short, fat man had Terrell's respect. They had worked together for a long time and Terrell valued Lowis's work and his opinions.

'You got something, doc?' he asked as the two men carried the stretcher out.

'I guess so,' Lowis returned. 'This is supposed to be the murder weapon.' He pointed to the leg of a chair, lying on a strip of plastic on the table. 'There are blood and brains on it. At first sight, it is obviously the murder weapon, but I can't see how it can be. The man's skull was smashed. The weapon that inflicted such an injury must have been something like a loaded cosh . . . even a steel bar. To have hit a man that hard would have broken the chair leg.'

Terrell looked at Hess, a thickset man with a round face and granite hard eyes.

'You got anything, Fred?'

'Doc's right. I go along with his theory. And another thing . . . there are no prints on the chair leg. Whoever handled it wore gloves.'

Terrell pulled at his thick nose while he thought.

'Why should Forrester have worn gloves?' he asked eventually. 'Did he own a pair of gloves?'

'I asked,' Hess said. 'No . . . he had no gloves.'

'Could he have wiped the chair clean of prints?'

Why should he? Anyway, the chair leg hasn't been wiped. There are blood smears right up the leg.'

Again Terrell paused to think, then he said, 'Any of his clothes missing?'

'A blue tropical suit, a shirt, underwear, socks and shoes. I got Mason to check the closet.'

Terrell looked at the broken chair lying on its side in the corner of the room.

'No prints there?'

'No.'

'Okay . . . take the chair. We'll experiment with it. Let's see how the other legs stand up to a real heavy blow.'

While Hess was instructing one of his men to take care of the chair, Terrell joined Beigler in the hall below.

'Anything, Joe?'

'Nothing much. I've talked to the gate-man. He was asleep, but he thinks he heard a car start up during the night. He won't swear to it, and he didn't look at the time.'

'A car? What would a car be doing up here in the night? It's a cul-de-sac.'

'He won't swear to it.'

'It's important, Joe. If he did hear a car, then it looks as if Forrester had outside help. It's going to make the hunt for him much more tricky.'

'Doc thinks Lewis was killed around two o'clock. That would give Forrester a two hour start. If he had a car, the road blocks are now so much waste of time.'

'Could be he had outside help. The murder weapon bothers me. Lewis's skull was cracked open. How did Forrester get hold of a weapon that could inflict such an injury and why did he try to make us believe the injury was caused by the chair leg?'

The noise of a droning helicopter made both men look at each other, then they moved to the front door and walked out into the grey light of the dawn.

'Williams has been quick,' Terrell said as both men watched a low flying helicopter with U.S. Army markings, sweeping around the mansion. 'I have an idea this is also a waste of time. If Forrester had a car, then he is miles away by now.'

Beigler said, 'Do we put out a five State alarm, Chief?'

'I'll have to ask Williams. I'll get back to headquarters. If we send out an alarm, the press will pick it up. It'll make headlines around the world. Forrester is important. Keep digging, Joe. We want every lead we can find.'

Terrell arrived back at headquarters soon after six a.m. He went to his office, called for coffee and then for Max Jacoby.

'Anything?' he asked as the young detective came in.

'Routine stuff, sir,' Jacoby said. 'A woman found dead. She worked at the Go-Go Club. She left the bar drunk and fell into the harbour.'

'Don't bother me with that. Give it to Lepski,' Terrell said impatiently, 'Anything on Forrester?'

'No, sir.'

The telephone bell began to ring and Terrell waved Jacoby away. He picked up the receiver.

'This is Mervin Warren, calling from Washington,' a voice told him. 'I'll be down by midday. I'm sending Jesse Hamilton from the C.I.A. ahead of me. He should be with you pretty soon. Have you any news for me?'

Terrell knew Mervin Warren only by reputation. He knew he was the head of Rocket Research and very V.I.P. He had also heard he was a good man to deal with. He instilled a little deference into his voice as he told Warren of Dr. Lowis's theory about the murder weapon and added the gate-man had thought he had heard a car.

'Williams of the F.B.I. has started an overhead search, sir,' Terrell went on. 'There are two helicopters right now searching the desert. We have road blocks set up.'

'I don't have to tell you,' Warren said, his voice anxious, 'that Forrester is important . . . top priority. We have to find him.'

'Yes, I understand. How about the press?'

'We must use the press. Hamilton is bringing with him photographs of Forrester. I want them printed on the front page of every newspaper. From what you tell me it is remotely possible that he has been kidnapped. The Russian and the Chinese Governments would give a lot to get him in their hands. We've got to find him fast.' He paused, then went on, 'Let Hamilton handle the press. Don't allow any of your men to give out with information. This must be handled right. The press must only be allowed censored information and Hamilton knows what to tell them. Have a car for me at the airport. I'll be on the 589 flight,' and he hung up.

Terrell brooded for some minutes, then he pulled a big pad towards him and began to make notes.

Detective 2nd Grade Tom Lepski was regarded by his colleagues as a bit of a hellion, always kicking against discipline, but first class in his job once he got his teeth into a case. He was a tall wiry man, tough, with a lined sun-tanned face and clear ice-blue eyes, and he was ambitious.

He reached headquarters, after the emergency call had gone out, soon after six o'clock. He was in a vile temper as he had promised his wife he would take her down to the beach for the day, this being his day off duty, and now he found himself back on duty again.

He had left his wife also in a vile temper.

If he had been assigned to the search for Forrester, he wouldn't have minded so much as he was sure the press would very soon get on to the case, and every detective engaged in the search would sooner or later see a photograph of himself in the papers. His wife liked nothing better than to see a photograph of her husband's lean features in her local paper. This gave her tremendous kudos with her neighbours, and besides, Lepski himself was a publicity hunter.

When Jacoby, looking worn and heavy eyed, handed Lepski the report on the finding of Drena French's body and told him the Chief had said he was to take care of the investigation, Lepski nearly exploded.

'You mean you dragged me off my bed just to check on the death of some goddam whore?' he snarled.

Jacoby liked and admired Lepski. He kept his face straight as he said, 'If you've got a beef, Tom, take it up with the Chief. I'm only acting on orders.'

Lepski snorted.

'And all the dead-weights, all the pin-heads on this Force are looking for Forrester . . . right?'

'All the dead-weights and all the pin-heads,' Jacoby said, shaking his head. 'Detective 2nd Grade Lepski has been picked for the plum job. My congratulations.'

'There are times when I think the Chief should retire,' Lepski said in disgust. 'He at least needs his head examined.' He folded the report and stuffed it into his hip pocket. 'And take that smug look off your face!'

As Jacoby regarded him with a dead-pan expression, Lepski snorted and stamped out of the Detectives' room.

He drove fast to the waterfront. By the time he had reached the harbour, he had forgotten his grievance and had become the alert, quizzing cop that he was.

He found two patrolmen standing over a body covered with a rubber sheet, bored expressions on their faces. Mike O'Shane, a vast Irish cop, knew the waterfront like the back of his hand. The other cop, Dick Lawson, was less experienced and younger. He had been patrolling with O'Shane now for the past six months. It was to O'Shane that Lepski turned for information.

'That her?' he said and lifted aside the rubber sheet. He stared down at Drena's dead face. His experienced eyes told him that she had died before she could have drowned. The ragged wound across the side of her face was lethal. He grunted, then said to Lawson, 'Get the wagon and get her to the morgue.'

At this hour the harbour was still deserted and the three men had the place to themselves.

'Someone hit her, Mike?' Lepski asked.

'I don't think so. Look here . . .' O'Shane led him to the edge of the harbour and pointed to a dinghy. 'I reckon she fell off the harbour and caught her head against the dinghy . . . you can see the blood smear.'

Lepski regarded the blood marks on the white prow of the dinghy and grunted. He took hold of O'Shane's arm.

'Come over to the car and let's smoke,' he said. 'Dick can handle her.'

The big Irishman followed Lepski to his car and got into the passenger's seat. Lepski got into the driving seat. When he was sure Patrolman Lawson had gone over to a distant telephone booth to call the ambulance, he took a half pint bottle of whisky from his glove compartment and offered it to O'Shane whose small eyes widened. He needed no second invitation. He took a long, generous drink, sighed, wiped the neck of the bottle with his sleeve and handed it back to Lepski.

'Fine whisky,' he said.

Lepski didn't take a drink himself. He returned the bottle to the glove compartment, offered a cigarette and took one himself. Both men lit up.

'What can you tell me about her, Mike?'

'She's Drena French: works at the Go-Go Club. Been there the past eighteen months. She has a room at 187, Anchor Street. I've never had trouble with her. I guess she must have been a little high and wandered off the harbour and fell in. She drank a lot.'

Lepski sighed. A hell of a dull case to get landed with, he thought, but he knew from long experience that a death like this was not always so easily explained.

'Did she have a boy-friend?'

'Yeah . . . he turned up at the club pretty near every night. Nice guy . . . I heard he works for the Harrison Wentworth Nut house . . . he's a male nurse.'

Lepski stiffened, turned in his seat to stare at O'Shane.

'He's a male nurse at the Harrison Wentworth?' he repeated. 'You sure?'

'So I heard.'

'Do you know his name?'

'Lewis? Could be . . . yeah, Lewis.'

Lepski picked up the telephone receiver in his car. He got through to Jacoby. 'Max . . . what's the name of the male nurse who got knocked off at the Nut house?'

'I thought you were supposed to be working on that woman in the harbour,' Jacoby said.

'You heard me!' Lepski bawled. 'What's his name?'

'Fred Lewis.'

Lepski replaced the receiver. He sat for some moments, staring into space while O'Shane regarded him curiously, then Lepski said, 'Who were her friends, Mike?'

'Friends? Well, a girl like her doesn't have friends. She got on all right with O'Brien . . . he runs the Club. A couple of times when she and I chewed the rag together, she mentioned the barman Tin-Tin Washington. He's a Jamaican. She seemed to think a lot of him . . . not a bad guy . . . never in trouble, but friends . . .' O'Shane shook his head.

'This Jamaican . . . know where I can find him?'

'Sure. He has a room right over there.' O'Shane pointed a thick finger. 'In that house.'

There came a wail of a siren and an ambulance appeared. It pulled up by Lawson and two interns scrambled out.

'Okay, Mike, you take over,' Lepski said. 'Get her to the morgue. I'll be over in a while. Tell Lawson to guard that dinghy. It's not to be moved.'

'Thanks for the drink,' O'Shane said. 'That's set me up. Okay, I'll handle it,' and leaving the car, he went over with heavy, plodding feet to the ambulance.

Lepski picked up the telephone receiver. When he got Jacoby he said, 'I want a photographer down here, Max. You got any spare Homicide men around? I want them too.'

'There's Macklin . . . the rest are up at the Nut house. What's cooking, Tom?'

'Send Macklin and a photographer pronto,' Lepski said and hung up.

He left the car and walked to the building indicated by O'Shane. It was a typical cheap lodging house that infested the harbour district. The old, dirty-looking man, dozing behind the desk, started awake as Lepski walked in. He recognized Lepski and his bleary old eyes became alarmed.

'Hello there, Captain,' he said, his voice anxious. 'You ain't looking for trouble?'

'Have you got trouble?' Lepski asked. Before he had become a detective, he had had a stint on the waterfront in uniform and knew most of the 'oldies' and they knew him.

'No, Captain . . . everything is as peaceful as a sleeping babe.'

'Yeah . . . a two headed monster . . . I know.'

The old man smirked uneasily.

'No trouble, Captain . . . I swear it.'

'Where do I find Tin-Tin Washington?'

'You wouldn't want him, Captain,' the old man said, his eyes bulging. 'The most peaceful . . .'

'Cut it out!' Lepski barked in his cop voice. 'Where do I find him?'

'Top floor . . . the door facing the stairs. He's been sleeping for the past three hours.'

Lepski started to climb the stairs. His temper was considerably frayed by the time he had reached the fifth and last landing. He hammered on the door facing him, waited, then banged again. He heard sounds of movement, then the door opened. The big Jamaican, wearing only a shirt, blinked at him, then recognizing a cop when he saw one, backed into the small, neatly kept room.

Lepski followed him in, looking around, approved of what he saw, then sat down on an upright chair.

'Relax,' he said. He knew the waterfront people. When you could, you treated them with kid gloves. You got more out of them that way. 'Sorry to wake you, fella. We've got trouble. You could help.'

Tin-Tin gave a great gaping yawn, rubbed his eyes, groaned, then shook his head.

'Man! You've got nothing like the trouble I have . . . I'm dead right here on my feet.' He shook his head again, then walked over to a hot plate on which stood a blackened coffee pot. 'You want coffee? I keep it always hot. Man! Do I want coffee!'

'Why not? Lepski said and lit a cigarette.

As Tin-Tin poured two cups of black coffee, he said, 'What's the trouble, mister? Lemme see . . . you're Tom Lepski, ain't you? Used to pound a beat down here four-five years ago?'

'That's right,' Lepski said. 'But I've moved up in the world.' He grinned as he accepted the cup of coffee. 'Detective 2nd Grade . . . I'll be Chief in another five years.'

Tin-Tin sat on the bed. He drank some of the coffee, sighed, then putting down the cup, he began to scratch his bony knees.

'Yeah . . . could be. Old Mike speaks well of you. He knows.' Then he stopped scratching and looked inquiringly at Lepski. The drink of coffee had brought him awake. 'I've got to be at the Club by one o'clock this afternoon. I'd like some sleep. You want something from me, Mr. Lepski?'

'You know Drena French?'

Tin-Tin stiffened.

'Sure I know her. She and me are good friends. Is she in trouble?'

'You could call it that. Would you say she was drunk last night?'

'Drunk? Well, no. A little high, but not drunk. Has something happened to her?'

'She was picked out of the harbour: smashed head . . . dead as an amputated leg.'

Tin-Tin wilted.

'You mean she's dead?'

'Yeah . . . dead.'

A sadness came into the Jamaican's enormous black eyes that made Lepski look away. Tin-Tin sat for some seconds staring down at the threadbare mat on which his splayed, naked feet rested. Then he drew in a long breath. 'Well, that's the way it is, mister. Here, one day . . . gone, the next. I guess Jesus will take care of her.'

'I guess.' Lepski finished his coffee. 'What do you know about her boy-friend . . . Fred Lewis?'

'Not much. He was a non-drinking man. He just came and sat. I do know he was crazy about the girl . . . you watch a man . . . you see how he reacts . . . there's that light in his eyes. Yes, Man, he sure was crazy about her.'

Lepski pushed his empty cup towards Tin-Tin.

'Can you spare any more . . . it's damn fine coffee.'

This pleased Tin-Tin. He got off the bed and refilled Lepski's cup.

'Glad you like it, Mr. Lepski . . . I reckon it's pretty good myself and I reckon I'm a pretty good judge.'

There was a pause, then Lepski said, 'Odd combination . . . these two . . . a male nurse and a whore.'

'You think so?' Tin-Tin shook his head. 'Not to me. Folks find each other: they get together: they click. I've seen it time after time.'

'She had been drinking?'

Tin-Tin hesitated, then nodded.

'Well, I guess. It's a real tough life for a girl at the Club. She has to keep on the ball. Yeah, sure . . . she had been drinking.'

'She wouldn't have tossed herself into the harbour? She wasn't unhappy?'

'Unhappy?' Tin-Tin showed his big white teeth like piano keys in the overhead light. 'Nothing like that . . . she told me she was going to own a restaurant. Okay, she must have been high, but she was happy. No, mister, she didn't jump. That I'll swear.'

'What's this about a restaurant?'

'Well, you know how these girls shoot with the mouth. She told me she was buying the Seagull. You know it? It's a dead beat joint on Eastern Point. She said she and her boy-friend were buying it. She said last night was her last night at the Club. Women! They shoot with their mouths. I guess she was a little high.' Tin-Tin sighed. 'Now, she's dead.'

Lepski knew The Seagull Restaurant. He knew the owner, Jeff Hawkins. He also knew that Hawkins wanted to sell and why. Here was an interesting lead. He got to his feet.

'Okay, Tin-Tin,' he said. 'Sorry to have woken you up. You get back to bed.'

'She said everything was on the house if I came around,' Tin-Tin said sadly. 'Well, Mr. Lepski, she could have been drunker than I thought.'

'Yeah. You get back to sleep and thanks for the coffee . . . best coffee I've had in years,' and Lepski meant just that.

He left the room, took the stairs two at the time and walked out on to the sunlit waterfront. Already amateur yachtsmen were getting their boats ready for a morning sail. Lepski went over to Patrolman Lawson who was standing guard by the bloodstained dinghy.

'Homicide will be down any moment now,' he said. 'That boat doesn't move until they've looked at it. Understand?'

Awed by Lepski's reputation, Lawson saluted.

'Yes, sir,' he said.

Lepski got into his car and drove along the waterfront. Eventually, he arrived outside The Seagull Restaurant. He got out of the car and stared at the run-down building, then walked to the locked door. He hammered on the door panel until, after a long delay, the door swung open.

Jeff Hawkins, elderly, wearing a dirty white bath-robe, his big feet in sandals, gaped sleepily at him.

'For the love of Mike! It's Chief of Police Lepski!' he exclaimed.

'Not yet,' Lepski said, pleased. 'How are you, Jeff? Long time no see.'

'Yeah. I was asleep. Anything wrong?'

'Always trouble,' Lepski said and shouldered his way past the big man into the dark, shabby restaurant. 'Let's have a light.'

Hawkins flicked on an overhead light. A woman's shrill voice bawled down from upstairs to know what was happening. Hawkins bawled up, telling her to shut her mouth. There was silence.

Lepski leaned on the small bar, looking at Hawkins who looked around rather helplessly. He was still stunned by sleep.

'Do you want coffee, Captain?'

'Nothing. You selling this dump?'

Hawkins brightened.

'It's sold. That little tart from the Go-Go Club: Drena French. She's paying me seven thousand bucks. Boy! Am I glad to get rid of it!' Seeing Lepski's cop expression, he stiffened and asked, 'Something wrong? Hasn't she the money? I kept asking myself how a whore like her could find that amount of money, but she swore by her mother's grave she was signing the papers today.'

'Well, she won't,' Lepski said. 'It's your hard luck, Jeff. We've fished her out of the harbour.'

Hawkins' big, sweaty face sagged. 'Dead?'

'Yeah.'

The big man sank on to a stool. He rubbed his fleshy, work-hardened hand over his face.

'Well, that's the way it is,' he said. 'I really thought I had got out.'

Lepski took out his notebook.

'Let's have all the details, Jeff,' he said. 'Right from the time she propositioned you.'

CHAPTER FOUR

IT WAS BY the merest chance that Jonathan Lindsey was in the lobby of the Belvedere Hotel when a secretary, calling from Washington, asked for a reservation for Mervin Warren.

Lindsey was feeling pretty satisfied. The first stage of the operation had succeeded. They now had Paul Forrester. They had his one time assistant, Nona Jacey. There were no loose ends. Silk and Keegan had done a smooth, efficient job. He had already sent a Telex to the Alcron Hotel, Prague, where Radnitz was staying, alerting Radnitz in code of the progress so far.

Now he was waiting to hear that Dr. Alex Kuntz had been safely taken to the cave hideout. While he was waiting, he examined the Stock list in the *New York Times,* and it was while he was trying to decide whether or not to increase his holdings in Com Sat that he heard the receptionist talking on the telephone say, 'Mr. Mervin Warren? Yes, of course. A suite? Yes, certainly. We'll be happy to have Mr. Warren. Yes . . . I understand. At midday? Certainly. Everything will be ready for him. Thank you . . . you're welcome,' and she hung up.

Lindsey glanced at his watch. The time was ten minutes after ten. His brain worked swiftly. Folding his newspaper, he got casually to his feet. He walked to the reception desk. The tall, slim girl, wearing a neat, sky blue dress, smiled at him.

'Good morning, Mr. Lindsey.'

Lindsey returned her smile. Charm radiated from him, making her eyes sparkle. Lindsey had this trick. Few women could resist that suave, admiring gaze.

'You are looking delightful, Miss Whitelaw,' he said. He had always made it a rule to know the names of the important members of the staff of all the hotels he frequented: something that baffled Radnitz who never bothered to remember anyone's name. 'That dress matches your eyes beautifully.'

The girl laughed, delighted. What all the girls working at the hotel liked about Lindsey was his charm and his kindness. They knew he would never make a pass, never take advantage of their position. They considered him to be quite the nicest client in the hotel which was what Lindsey wanted them to think.

'I couldn't help overhearing what you were saying just now,' Lindsey said with an apologetic smile. 'Mr. Warren is a very old friend of mine. I hope you are giving him a good suite?'

'Oh yes, Mr. Lindsey. He'll be in suite 875. It is the best, after Mr. Radnitz's suite.'

'I know it. Good . . .' Lindsey smiled, nodded and moved slowly away. He took the elevator to the penthouse suite, entered, walked to a desk and opened a drawer. From it he took a small square-shaped box. From the box he took what looked like a black plastic button. He dropped it into his pocket. Leaving the suite, he went down the stairs to the next floor and walked slowly along the corridor.

In the Service room he found Josh, the Negro valet who looked after the penthouse suite.

'Good morning, Josh,' Lindsey said, pausing in the doorway. 'I would like to look at suite 875. Is it vacant?'

Josh turned, his black face beaming.

'Yes, sir . . . right now it's vacant, but someone's moving in after midday.'

'A friend of mine is coming this way next month,' Lindsey said smoothly. 'I just want to make sure he will be comfortable.'

'Yes, sir. You come with me. You see for yourself, sir.'

Lindsey followed the Negro down the corridor, waited until the Negro had unlocked the door to the suite, then as the Negro stood aside, Lindsey entered.

He looked around the big living-room with its terrace. At one end of the room was a long, rectangular table with eight chairs set around it. This would be where Mervin Warren would hold his conferences, Lindsey decided. He walked over to the table as Josh began to pull up the sunblinds, his back turned to him. Lindsey took the black button from his pocket and his hand disappeared under the table. The adhesive back of the button—a high powered microphone—stuck to the underpart of the table. The movement was made so quickly that the Negro was completely unaware of what had happened.

Lindsey casually inspected the three bedrooms, the three bathrooms, then returned to the living-room.

'Yes, this will do, Josh. Couldn't be better. Thank you.' A five dollar bill exchanged hands, then, smiling, Lindsey left the suite and returned to Radnitz's penthouse. Once there, he opened a closet where, on a shelf, stood a *Revox* tape recorder. He put on a reel of tape, then satisfied with his preparations, he walked out on to the terrace. He stood in the sunshine for some time, watching the distant helicopters circling vainly in their search for Paul Forrester.

Mervin Warren was a tall, massively built man with a shock of white hair, a dimpled chin and alert, penetrating black eyes. He had arrived at the Belvedere Hotel at twenty minutes past noon and fifteen minutes later was seated at the head of the table in his private suite.

Chief of Police Terrell was on his left. Jesse Hamilton of the Central Intelligence Agency on his right. Roger Williams of the Federal Bureau of Investigation further down the table and Alec Horn, his secretary, at the far end of the table, taking notes.

'Well, gentlemen,' Warren was saying, 'you have all read Captain Terrell's report. I would like your conclusions. Hamilton? What do you think?'

Jesse Hamilton, thin, balding, his eyes shrewd, his mouth revealing the determination and ruthlessness of his character, said without hesitation, 'This all points to a conspiracy. There are a number of facts in this report that proves that Forrester did not escape without outside help. The set-up, as Captain Terrell found it when he arrived at the sanatorium, looked as if Forrester had murdered his nurse, stolen the master key and had got away. Now we have had time to examine the report, it seems to me that the facts don't jell with what we are supposed to believe.' He leaned back in his chair and raised a finger. 'Fact one: the chair leg could not have killed Lewis. A much heavier weapon must have been used. Fact two: there were no fingerprints on the chair leg which was not wiped clean, showing the person handling the chair leg wore gloves. We know Forrester didn't have any gloves. Fact three: the gate-man claims to have heard a car start up some time during the night. This isn't evidence as he can't swear to it, but it adds to the picture. Fact four: we now learn that the male nurse, Fred Lewis, was infatuated by a woman, working at a night club. Lewis went often to the Club. Suddenly this woman tells the barman at the Club that she is about to buy a restaurant. Fact five: the owner of this restaurant admits the woman made an offer of seven thousand dollars for the place. How could she find such a sum? Was this money coming from Lewis? Did he get the money as a bribe? Fact six: both Lewis and the woman are dead. The woman is supposed to have fallen into the harbour. But did she? Her head was smashed against a boat. If she had fallen naturally, could she have received such an injury? Dr. Lowis thinks she was thrown into the harbour with considerable violence. Lewis had his skull split by a very heavy weapon . . . this weapon hasn't been found. So, looking at the evidence, I am inclined to think that Forrester had outside help and an attempt has been made to make us believe that he escaped on his own. As Forrester was our top Rocket scientist, I would say that he has been kidnapped.'

There was a pause, then Warren looked at Roger Williams, a short, lean man with thinning blond hair and a heavy suntan.

'What do you think?'

'I go along with Hamilton,' Williams said. 'This is much too slick. Yes . . . I'd say the chances are Forrester has been kidnapped.'

Warren turned to Terrell.

'And you?'

Terrell rubbed his unshaven jaw. Since he had left home, he hadn't had a minute to spruce himself up.

'I don't know about kidnapping,' he said, 'but I'm sure there was outside help.'

Warren looked at his watch.

'I think Dr. Hertz should be here by now. We'll ask him in.'

His secretary left the room. A few moments later, he returned with Hertz.

'Come in, doctor,' Warren said, getting to his feet. He introduced each man, then waved Hertz to a chair. 'It would be helpful if you would tell us about how Forrester was last night . . . if he was behaving oddly and so on.'

Hertz sat down. He looked harassed and uneasy.

'His condition hasn't changed since he has been with me. He is always placid, refusing to mix with anyone, scarcely speaking. He is like a man in constant shock.'

'You had no hint that he could become violent?'

'No . . . but that doesn't mean he could not become violent at any moment. To put it simply, he is like a hand grenade with a faulty pin. Any kind of vibration could make the grenade explode.

'Both Lewis and Mason, his personal attendants, were well aware of this condition. They always approached him with caution.'

'How do you imagine he would react once he was out in the open?' Warren asked.

Hertz hesitated, frowning.

'That is hard to say. However, knowing his case history, it is likely he would try to find his wife. I have always known this brooding calm of his was connected with the memory of his wife. Here could be considerable danger. If he found her, the grenade could explode.'

Warren turned to Terrell.

'Do you know where his wife is?'

'She lives in a rented beach bungalow on Seaview Avenue,' Terrell told him.

Warren thought for a moment, then got to his feet.

'All right, doctor, we won't keep you any longer. This affair is now out of your hands.' He smiled. 'You can resume your normal duties and leave it to these gentlemen.'

Hertz stood up.

'I would like to say this has never happened before. I must, of course, accept responsibility . . .'

'That's all right, doctor,' Warren said quietly. 'No one is blaming you. Thank you for coming.'

His secretary edged Hertz out of the room. As soon as the door closed, Warren said, 'We must put a guard on Mrs. Forrester's bungalow at once.'

Terrell nodded and, going over to the telephone, he called headquarters. When he got Beigler, he said, 'We want a night and day guard on Mrs. Forrester's bungalow on Seaview Avenue. Get two good men down there right away. There's a chance Forrester might go there . . . warn them to keep on their toes.'

Above, in the penthouse, listening to all this and recording the conversation, Lindsey grimaced. So it hadn't been the slick, smooth operation he had planned. It seemed to be coming slightly unstuck at the seams. He reached for a boiled sweet, put it in his mouth, then sat forward in his chair as Warren began to talk again.

Warren said, 'If Forrester was kidnapped we don't want it known. This must be regarded as Top Secret. It is still possible someone helped him to escape and he wasn't kidnapped. It is possible he will try to find his wife. All this is something we must keep from the press. We could be lucky and use his wife as a trap to catch him. On no account is the press to be told about his wife or where she is. The press is only to be told that Forrester has escaped. In this way, if he has been kidnapped, his kidnappers will believe we don't suspect what has happened and they will be less on their guard.' He looked around the table. 'Do you all agree?'

Terrell said quietly, 'If we say Forrester has escaped, the press will naturally assume he killed his nurse. Do you want it that way?'

'For the moment it doesn't matter,' Warren said. 'We know that it is most unlikely he did kill Lewis. All this can be taken care of when we have found Forrester. What is important is for the people who have arranged his escape to believe we have accepted the scene as they have set it.'

'I don't think that quite hooks up with Terrell's point,' Williams said. 'Suppose Forrester is on the run . . . hasn't been kidnapped . . . and he reads in the papers he is suspect number one for Lewis's killing . . . how is he going to react?'

Terrell nodded to Hamilton. That was just the point he was making.

Warren frowned.

'I still think it is important that the press should believe Forrester escaped without help,' he said after a moment's hesitation. 'It is better for the public not to know that this could be a major international incident.'

Lindsey got to his feet. He thanked his stars he had planted the microphone in Warren's suite. He must alert Radnitz. This operation was suddenly becoming complicated. He began to feel uneasy. Was the cave hideout safe enough? Leaving the tape recorder to take care of the conversation still going on, he went to the desk and began to draft a Telex in code to Radnitz.

Sergeant Joe Beigler was once more in charge of the Detectives' room. Jacoby, with two men, had already left to guard Mrs. Forrester's bungalow. The search for Forrester was now out of the hands of the police. The F.B.I. and the Army had taken over.

Beigler was handling the usual routine work, a bored expression on his face.

Lepski was lolling at his desk, digging his penknife viciously into the battered desk top, watching Beigler, waiting for a lull. When the lull came, Lepski said, 'Joe, I'm a great dick. Look at the way I handled that whore's death. I should be up-graded. Did you see the Chief's face when I handed in my report . . . it stood him on his ear.'

Beigler was used to Lepski. He knew he was smart, but he also knew it would be some time before he was moved out of his Grade. Lepski was too much of a hustler . . . too publicity minded to make an early promotion.

'Just plain dumb luck,' he said, lighting a cigarette from the butt of the one he was smoking. 'All the same, Tom, you didn't do a bad morning's work. I wouldn't be surprised, once the news breaks, you'll be on the telly.'

Lepski sat up.

'You think that, Joe?' His lean face lit up. 'Sweet grief! That would kill Carroll! Yeah . . . you've got something! Me on television! My goddam neighbours would gnaw at their toe nails with envy.'

'Of course, the Chief might decide to go on instead of you,' Beigler said, keeping his face straight. 'He might say, "information from a report received . . ." You know how they word it, then no one would know our Sherlock Lepski was behind the whole *denouement*.'

Lepski gaped at him.

'The whole . . . what, for God's sake?'

'*Denouement*.'

'What the hell does that mean?'

'It's French.' Beigler looked smug. Baffled by the word he had come across in a paperback, he had looked it up in a dictionary. Now, he forced the word as often as he could into his day-to-day limited vocabulary. 'Don't worry your brains, Tom. What's a little education between a Sergeant and a 2nd Grade Detective?'

Lepski glared at him.

'Are you taking the mickey out of me, Joe?'

'Who—me? I wouldn't do that.'

'Yeah?' Lepski brooded for a moment, his face darkening. 'But you could be right. If anyone goes on the telly it will be the Chief. Boy! Does it burn me! I do the work . . .'

The telephone bell rang. Beigler scooped up the receiver, listened, then said, 'Okay, I'll send someone down. Yeah . . . right away,' and he hung up.

Lepski looked suspiciously at him.

'Not me again! I'm supposed to be on the beach with my goddam wife right at this very minute!'

Beigler looked around the big room, deliberately staring at each empty desk until his eyes alighted on Lepski.

'I can't see anyone else to send,' he said. 'That was the State Hospital. Olsen's just called. Alec Sherman is ready to talk. Olsen wants to know if he should take down Sherman's statement. Well, you know Olsen: he can't spell. You'd better get over. The *Herald* has been screaming blue murder about Sherman. You get a story from him, and they will spread your face bang across the front page.'

Lepski got out of his chair so fast, he knocked it over backwards.

'Yeah . . . you're right, Joe. I'm on my way. This could be my break into big time!'

With a concealed grin, Beigler watched his hurried departure, then turned back to the mass of reports still waiting his attention. The telephone bell rang. Sighing, he reached for the receiver.

While he was trying to soothe an agitated old lady whose cat had got wedged in a chimney, Lepski drove, with siren wailing, like a released rocket, down to the State Hospital.

He found Detective 3rd Grade Gustav Olsen flirting with a pert, good-looking nurse in the lobby of the hospital. Olsen, vast, with a red, good-natured face, would never make a great detective, but he was sound on routine. Lepski had long ago decided he had a lump of lead in his head for a brain, but when it came to a drag-out and a beat-up, Olsen was the best man on the Force.

For the past five days, Olsen had been sitting by the bed in which Alec Sherman, star reporter of the *Paradise Herald*, had been lying. The *Paradise Herald* had screamed its head off at the inefficiency of the police to allow any citizen—especially their star reporter—to have been so savagely beaten-up. Every day, they had nagged and nagged in their columns, demanding action. Under pressure, Terrell had planted Olsen by the unconscious man's bed to satisfy the newspaper that the moment Sherman could talk, action would be taken.

Seeing Lepski come striding across the lobby, Olsen sighed regretfully.

'Later, babe,' he said to the nurse. 'Here comes trouble. You and me will go somewhere, do something, some time soon.'

The girl looked at Lepski as he approached and she gave him a sexy smile. Lepski ignored her. All he was thinking about was a two column picture of himself on the front page of the *Herald*.

'Is he talking?' he asked, grabbing Olsen's arm.

'He's come to the surface,' Olsen told him. 'I didn't want to spoil it for you. Doc says only five minutes . . . no more. The poor bastard is in a bad way.'

Lepski patted his shoulder.

'You did right. You get back to that nurse. You leave this to me,' and he took the elevator to the fourth floor.

Lepski knew Alec Sherman. He made it his business to know all the newspaper reporters in the City. When he entered the small room, he was shocked to see the bandaged wreck that lay in the bed. Most of Sherman's face was concealed by bandages. One eye peered out of the mask of white lint and Lepski felt a surge of angry indignation run through him.

'Hello, pal,' he said quietly and drew up a chair. 'The doc

says you can only talk for five minutes . . . don't let's waste time. Did you see who did it?'

'No . . . I got in my car and got hit on the head,' Sherman said, speaking with difficulty. His broken jaw was wired and every movement, when trying to speak, hurt him. 'Look, Tom, I'm worried sick. I haven't heard from Nona . . . she's my girl. Will you check on her? The nurse tells me she hasn't been here nor even telephoned. She must have heard what happened to me. Fod God's sake, Tom . . . please check on her.'

Lepski contained his impatience with an effort. He didn't want to be bothered with Sherman's girl . . . what he was after was a story that would put him on the front page of the *Herald*.

'Sure, sure . . . I'll check on her. Now, tell me . . . you never even saw who hit you?'

Sherman's visible eye closed. He lay still for a long moment, then, making the effort, he said, 'I saw nothing. Tom . . . please. Her name is Nona Jacey. She lives at 1890 Lexington Road. She works at the Rocket Research Station. Will you please find out why she hasn't been asking after me?'

Lepski stiffened. For a moment he couldn't believe what he was hearing.

'The Rocket Research Station?' he repeated, awe in his voice.

'That's right. She was Paul Forrester's assistant a couple of years back. I'm worried about her. We are going to be married.' Sherman was breathing heavily. The effort of talking was making him sweat.

Lepski was already on his feet. His eyes alight with excitement.

'1890 Lexington Road . . . right?'

'Yes.'

'Take it easy . . . I'm on my way. I'll let you know what's happening,' and Lepski rushed out of the room.

Paul Forrester's assistant! he thought as he took the elevator down to the ground floor. Could he have stumbled on something? As the doors of the elevator swished open, he started across the lobby. Olsen was still talking to the nurse. Lepski swept past him, rushing down the steps to his car.

Olsen stared after him.

'Now that's a fink who can't take it easy,' he said, smiling at the nurse. 'But I'm a guy with a big talent.'

She giggled.

'The bigger the better.' She gave him a long, inviting stare, then went on, 'I must get back to work. Tonight?'

Olsen grinned happily.

'I'm signing off at eight. You and me will go places and I'll show you something that'll surprise you.'

'I can imagine.' She turned and hip-swished her way along the corridor.

Lepski pulled up outside 1890 Lexington Road. He got out of his car and hurried up the steps. He entered the lobby, examined the mail boxes, saw that Nona Jacey had an apartment on the third floor. He checked his watch. The time was twenty minutes to one p.m. The girl wouldn't be in her apartment. If she was anywhere she would be at work. He looked around, saw the notice with the arrow, pointing to Mrs. Watson's apartment. He crossed the lobby and rang the bell. There was a delay, then the door opened and Mrs. Watson regarded him with her cold hostility.

'What is it?' she demanded.

In his time, Lepski had interviewed hundreds of landladies. He knew just how to handle them. This old bag, he told himself, had to be handled carefully. He lifted his hat, then produced his badge.

'Police, madam,' he said. 'I think you can help me.'

Mrs. Watson examined the badge, then she scowled at Lepski.

'I've no trouble here, mister,' she said and began to close the door.

'It's not trouble, madam,' Lepski said. 'I'm looking for Miss Jacey.'

Mrs. Watson's face turned sour.

'That little thief! She left a week ago! Good riddance!'

Lepski leaned his frame against the door post making it impossible for Mrs. Watson to close the door.

'Thief? I didn't know. What makes you say that?'

'You, the police, and don't know?' Mrs. Watson's tone was scathing.

'If I kept tabs on everyone in this city, madam, I'd never do any work,' Lepski said. 'What happened?'

Mrs. Watson told him with relish. Lepski listened.

'Her cousin from Texas came four days ago and took her things . . . good riddance,' Mrs. Watson concluded.

'Her cousin?'

'That's right . . . a chit of a girl. She said she was taking Jacey back with her to Texas.'

'Did she give her name?'

Mrs. Watson screwed up her face as she thought.

'Sheila Mason,' she said finally. 'Yes . . . Sheila Mason.'

'Did she give an address?'

'No . . . why should I want her address?'

'Can you give me a description of her?' Lepski asked, taking out his notebook.

'She was blonde . . . blue eyes . . . a chit . . . no better than she should be. Those mini-skirts. If I had a daughter who dared to wear one of those skirts I'd fill her bottom with shoe leather!' Mrs. Watson declared, folding her arms and looking righteous.

Lepski, a great fan of mini-skirts, grunted.

'Age?'

'I don't know . . . twenty-three . . . twenty-four . . .'

Lepski asked further questions, then, satisfied that he had all the information he would get from the woman, he raised his hat and went back to his car. He drove to the nearest drug-store and telephoned the State Hospital. After some delay, he got through to Detective Olsen.

'Listen, hunk-head,' Lepski said once he had Olsen on the line, 'ask Sherman if he knows anything about Nona Jacey's cousin from Texas. Her name's Sheila Mason. You listening?'

He could hear Olsen's laboured breathing over the line. Olsen said he was listening.

'You haven't got your hand up that nurse's skirt?' Lepski demanded suspiciously.

'What are you talking about?' Olsen said indignantly. 'She's nowhere near me!'

'Your bad luck . . . now, listen . . . go up to Sherman and ask him . . . Nona Jacey's cousin . . . what does he know about her.'

Lepski had to repeat the names three times before he was sure Olsen had got them right, then Olsen told him to hold on.

Lepski smoked three cigarettes and was half out of his mind with impatience before Olsen came back on the line.

'Sherman says this Nona dame hasn't a cousin . . . she hasn't any relations. You stringing me or something?'

'You're sure he said that?' Lepski demanded.

'That's what the guy said . . . no cousin . . . no relations. I guess she's lucky.'

Lepski hung up. He went back to his car and drove fast to the Court House. It took him a good half hour to get all the details of Nona's arrest, her trial and her sentence. By now he had been out of touch with headquarters for two hours. He knew Beigler would be wondering what he was doing. Reluctantly, he went to a phone booth and called headquarters.

'Listen, Joe,' he said when Beigler came on the line. 'I'm on to something big. I want a couple of hours and then I'll stand the Chief on both his ears!'

'You come right back!' Beigler growled. 'I've no one here and I've got a flock of work lined up for you. You come back here . . . hear me?'

'No,' Lepski said recklessly. 'I've bust my ear-drum,' and he hung up.

Twenty minutes later, he pulled up outside the Women's House of Correction. He had roared along the highway at ninety-five miles an hour, his siren wailing and he was sweating slightly as he got out of the car. He had had two horribly close escapes from a smash-up which had shaken him.

He knew the gate-man of the prison who in the past had pounded a beat with him. He talked to him. He was lucky that the bus that took released prisoners to the city was parked nearby and he talked to the bus driver. He heard about Lu-Lu Dodge. He got her address from the prison records. He drove back to the city, again at a break-neck speed. He found Lu-Lu Dodge after an hour's exasperating search. She was in a downtown bar, hopefully looking around for trade. He talked to her. She not only gave him an accurate description of the two men who had taken Nona Jacey away, but she also found in her bag, scribbled on the back of an old bill, the number of the car.

He got back to headquarters a little after four o'clock to find Beigler coping with the routine work with the aid of three rookie patrolmen he had called off their beats.

'All right . . . all right,' Lepski said, rushing into the Detectives' room. 'I know . . . you don't have to tell me. Boy! Have I something! Where's the Chief?'

Beigler clenched his massive fists.

'You're on your way out, Lepski,' he snarled. 'I've reported you. If you're not busted right off the Force, I'll . . .'

'Don't say it,' Lepski said. 'You'll regret it. Where's the Chief?'

Beigler pointed to Captain Terrell's door.

'It might surprise you to hear that the Chief is asking for you,' he said with heavy sarcasm. 'Go in there and get busted!'

Lepski grinned.

'You wait . . . Sherlock Lepski is really behind the whole doonooant!'

'Denouement . . . honk-head!' Beigler snarled. 'Get in there!'

The rented beach bungalow in which Thea Forrester lived had two bedrooms and a large living-room. It was set in a protective screen of palm trees and flowering shrubs. It was a love nest typical of those that abound along the shore of the west side of Paradise City. Each bungalow had access to the beach and the sea and no one could look to see what went on or was able to lift a disapproving eyebrow.

Since Paul Forrester had been locked away, and once over her terror of her near murder, Thea had decided to remain in Paradise City. She had many friends in the City. She had a reasonable pension from the U.S. Government, and there were many men around who were more than willing to supplement this income for favours received.

Thea was a slut. She could never understand how she had come to marry Forrester, but she had. Perhaps she had thought he would eventually become the top scientist and would make a fortune. She was the first to admit that money was the most important thing in her life. There was nothing she wouldn't do for money. She knew men thirsted for her kind of beauty. This was merchandise she knew well how to sell. She was sensationally beautiful, and she spent hours grooming herself, visiting the best hairdresser in the City every day, taking Sauna baths, exercising, swimming and sun bathing . . . devoting most of her time to the perfection of her thirty-year-old body.

She was slightly above average height. Her hair, sable tinted, made a perfect contrast to her large, emerald green eyes. Her features were perfect: her body a sculptor's dream. She knew exactly the right clothes to wear. She was never brash: never thought of wearing a mini-skirt. The smouldering sexual invitation that glowed in her green eyes was much more exciting to men than any show of knees and thighs.

She had said often enough to her girl-friends when they had asked her advice whether to go mini-skirt or not: 'Well, honey, if you think *they* like to see all that fat . . . that expanse of flesh from the top of your stockings to your pants . . . the sight of your hams if you sit in a too low chair . . . your fanny if you bend to pick something up . . . if you *really* think men—I'm not talking about randy boys—find that attractive, then go ahead. From the knee to the ankle is the really sexy thing. From your knees to your arse is just woman's fat.'

Her friends had listened, grimaced and went out and bought mini-skirts. There were times, they decided, that Thea was square.

Detective 3rd Grade Max Jacoby arrived at the beach cabin soon after 11.15 a.m. With him he had Dick Harper and Phil

Bates: two young detectives who had just changed out of uniform into plain clothes. Jacoby got out of the car.

'Take a look around. You'll be here, out of sight, for the next seven hours.' He had already instilled into them the importance of the assignment. 'If Forrester shows up, take care of him. Watch it? This guy's V.I.P. He could be violent. He even could be armed. You've got to smother him . . . understand? He's not to be hurt. You've got to remember he is a nut.'

Harper, the taller of the two detectives, said, 'We've got it. Come on, Phil,' and they moved away across the sand to a nearby clump of shrubs.

Jacoby went to the front door and pressed the bell. He waited several minutes before the door opened. He caught his breath sharply, as most men did at the first sight of Thea Forrester. She was wearing a pink wrap which she held close to her curves. The colour set off her hair. She regarded Jacoby; her eyes running over his athletic body, and then she smiled. Her teeth were dazzlingly white. Her hip was slightly cocked against the door post. Her slim fingers let the wrap slip a little to reveal the golden curve of a breast.

Jacoby was a dedicated cop. He got back on balance quickly. He showed his badge.

'Excuse me, madam, I've come from headquarters. I've been instructed to guard your bungalow.'

Thea's smile faded. The green eyes hardened. She lifted an eyebrow. 'Police? Guard? What do you mean?'

'The news hasn't broken yet,' Jacoby said quietly. 'Dr. Forrester has escaped from the sanatorium.'

He was shocked to see the abrupt change in this glamorous looking woman. She seemed to shrivel; the green eyes went dull. Blood drained from behind the tan, leaving her skin blotchy and mottled.

'Paul?' Her voice was suddenly husky. 'He—he's escaped?'

'There's nothing to worry about, madam,' Jacoby said. 'You will have constant guards. I—'

'Oh, shut up!' She looked beyond him at the lonely expanse of sand and sea. 'Come in!' She turned and led the way into the big lounge.

Jacoby followed her and stood in the doorway of the lounge, looking around at the confusion that reigned in the room. It was obvious there had been a drinking party the previous evening. Empty glasses and bottles, ashtrays spilling over with butts and ash, a pink bra hanging over a chair back, playing cards scattered on the carpet and the stale smell of drink and sweat made up the picture.

Although Thea was immaculate in herself, she lived like the slut she was, not caring how her home looked. She had a Negro woman who came in in the afternoons to clean up and this woman soon realized that Thea had no standards and worked accordingly.

'How did he get out?' Thea demanded, swinging around and glaring at Jacoby.

'I don't know,' Jacoby said, having been warned by Beigler to give away no information. 'But he's out.'

'Can't anyone do right?' Thea's voice was shrill. She was now slowly recovering from the shock, and the colour was back in her face. 'They had him . . . why the hell couldn't they have kept him? He's dangerous! He's mad! Why haven't they caught up with him?'

'We are searching for him, madam,' Jacoby said. 'We'll find him, but Captain Terrell thought, as long as he is free, you should be guarded.'

Thea walked slowly around the lounge while she thought. She snatched up the pink bra and pushed it under a chair cushion.

'What happens if he comes here?' she asked, pausing to look at Jacoby.

'He will be caught. You will be guarded night and day. You have nothing to worry about.'

'But how could he know I am here?'

'Captain Terrell thought we shouldn't take any chances.'

Thea made an impatient movement.

'So I'm to have two snoopers watching me?' She suddenly realized what this could mean and her eyes flashed angrily.

'They won't interfere with your privacy, madam,' Jacoby assured her. 'They are only here to guard you.'

'God!' Thea struck her hands together with exasperation. She had now recovered from her fright and was furious. 'Well, get on with it. Leave me alone!'

'Could I look over the bungalow, madam?' Jacoby asked. 'I would like to check the windows and the doors.'

'Not now . . . later,' Thea said. 'For heaven's sake, get out!'

'Very well, madam,' Jacoby said, slightly startled, and he left the bungalow.

Thea moved to the window and watched him through the grubby nylon curtains. She saw him walk off across the sand towards a clump of shrubs. Turning, she went quickly into the bedroom.

She found Bruce Adkin sitting on the edge of the double bed, struggling into a shortie dressing-gown. His tanned handsome face with its thin straight nose, its pencil-lined moustache and its thin sensual mouth wore an expression of alarm.

Adkin, a croupier at the Paradise City's Casino, had moved into the beach cabin some months ago. He was convenient to Thea. He worked at night and gave her the male companionship she needed during the day. The men she received at night never moved her, although she pretended they did. But Adkin had the technique her body required. He was one of the very few men who had the stamina and the endurance to give her complete satisfaction.

'Who was that?' he asked, standing up and tying the cord of the dressing-gown around his waist. He ran fingers through his black hair. He felt overhung. The previous evening had been one hell of a party. He had been completely plastered and now he had a vague recollection of having two women in bed with him.

'The police! Paul escaped last night!' Thea exclaimed. 'Those goddam fools have let him escape!'

Adkin stiffened. His bleary eyes widened.

'You mean your husband? That nut? He's escaped?'

'Yes! Now, I have a police guard. God! I could kill the fools!'

'You mean he's coming here?' Adkin turned pale.

'How the hell do I know? How could he know I'm here?'

'Then why the cops?'

'Don't keep asking stupid questions. Get me a drink! This has been a shock. Don't you understand that?'

'A shock? What do you think it's doing to me?' Adkin shouted. 'I'm getting out of here! Do you imagine I want a knife in my guts? I know what that nut did to your other boy-friend. Do you think I want my guts hanging out? I'm off. From now on, baby, you keep clear of me! I'm not tangling with some madman and getting my guts spread over the floor. That's strictly for the birds, but not for me!'

'You are not going to leave me here alone?' Thea asked, staring at him.

'You've got the cops.' Adkin was throwing on his clothes. 'They'll keep you company. If that nut found me here . . . oh, no! You stick with the cops. I'm getting out!'

Thea regarded him contemptuously.

'I knew you were soft, Bruce, but I didn't think you were that yellow.'

Adkin zipped up his trousers.

'Me . . . yellow? You don't know the half of it. I'm yellow right through to my marrow. When it comes to a nut with a knife, I'm more than yellow.'

She hesitated, then shrugged and walked into the lounge. She poured herself a stiff whisky. She drank it, shuddered, then lit a cigarette, irritated to see her hands were shaking. Perhaps after all it would be better for Bruce to get out, she decided. She couldn't afford another scandal if she wished to remain in Paradise City. Pretty soon the press would find her and it wouldn't do for them to find Bruce with her. Then she remembered that Wallace Marsh, the President of the local bank, was coming out to see her this night. She couldn't let him come with two cops watching the bungalow. She suddenly realized what a bodyguard meant. Her men friends—all married—used the bungalow because it was private and isolated. They had a horror of being seen with her in public. She sat down abruptly. This would mean she would be short of money. She had a flock of debts. She had planned to make at least six hundred dollars from her men friends by the end of the week.

Now, she didn't dare have them here. She would have to telephone them and make excuses. Excuses? Once they read the papers, they would know the truth and they would drop her like a red-hot brick.

Adkin came out of the bedroom, carrying a suitcase.

'I'm on my way, baby,' he said. 'Have a ball with the cops.'

She didn't bother to look at him. Her mind was too busy trying to decide what her next move should be.

She heard the front door slam, then a car start up and roar away. Getting to her feet, she went over to the telephone and began to cancel her dates.

At one p.m., the news broke that Dr. Paul Forrester, top U.S. Rocket Research scientist who had been two years in a sanatorium following a mental breakdown, had escaped.

The local TV station interrupted its programme to put Dr. Forrester's photograph on the screens of the City's TV viewers. The local radio station broadcast the news. The *Paradise Herald* rushed out a special edition that was on the streets by two-thirty. The public were asked to look out for Forrester.

'Don't attempt to apprehend this man,' the radio announcer

warned. 'He is believed violent. You should call Police Headquarters: telephone number: Paradise City 7777.'

Jesse Hamilton of the C.I.A. was given the job of handling the press. He set up his headquarters at the City Hall. So far the news hadn't leaked that Mervin Warren was on the scene, and Warren kept to his hotel suite. It was to the hotel that Terrell, Williams of the F.B.I. and Lepski rushed in a police car.

Lepski's report satisfied Terrell that there must be a conspiracy. Terrell now wanted Warren to have it first hand.

It was a great moment in Lepski's life when he recounted what he had done and heard during the past hours. Not only did Warren listen with absorbed interest, but also Jonathan Lindsey, sitting with headphones clamped to his ears in Radnitz's penthouse suite.

When Lepski had finished his report, Warren telephoned the Paradise Research Station. He had a brief conversation, then hung up.

'This Jacey girl would not have returned to work,' he told Terrell. 'Any employee convicted in Court automatically loses his or her job. So they didn't expect her back. I want to know if this girl Sheila Mason exists . . . if she lives in Texas. Can we find out?'

'I'll check, but we do know that Jacey had no relations so I very much doubt if Sheila Mason of Texas does exist, but I will check,' Terrell said.

'This store detective,' Warren went on. 'I want a check on him. We want to be absolutely sure that he did see Jacey steal the articles. If he is put under pressure he might admit he gave false evidence. This is important. If the girl was framed—and it looks as if she was—we would know for certain she is involved in the conspiracy.'

Terrell turned to Lepski.

'See him,' he said. 'If he doesn't talk, bring him to headquarters.'

Lepski got to his feet.

'Yes, sir,' he said and left the room.

Listening, Lindsey picked up the telephone receiver by his side. He asked for an outside line. When he got it, he dialled a number. Silk came on immediately.

'Emergency,' Lindsey said quietly. 'The police are on their way to interrogate that store detective. They could crack him. He could give them a description of you. Shut his mouth. They are on their way now, so hurry it up!'

As he replaced the receiver, he heard Warren say, 'These two men who met the Jacey girl when she was released. We must find them.'

'I'm working on that now,' Terrell said. 'We are looking for Lu-Lu Dodge. She had a good look at them. She is certain they were police officers. I know they weren't, but they could have been ex-police officers, working for some Agency. We have photographs of all ex-officers in our files. As soon as we pick her up, we'll get her to go through these photographs.'

Lindsey felt his hands grow damp. This was dangerous. If the police arrested the men from the Agency, they would talk. He was sure of that. He now felt a sense of panic. This operation was going wrong. The Agency would give the police his name. He didn't trust the man who ran it. He hesitated for a moment, then again dialled a number. This time Chet Keegan came on the line.

'The police are looking for a woman named Lu-Lu Dodge,' Lindsey told him. 'She can identify White and Fox. Get down to headquarters and wait for them to bring her in. Shut her mouth. Understand?'

'Lu-Lu Dodge? Sure . . . I know her,' Keegan said. 'Okay, I'm on my way,' and he hung up.

Lindsey then telephoned the Detective Agency.

'Get Fox and White down to Mexico,' he instructed. 'Pronto. I want them out of the State at once!'

'Okay,' a man's voice said, then his voice sharpened as he asked, 'Trouble?'

'Do what I tell you and don't ask questions!' Lindsey snapped.

When Lepski arrived at the Paradise Self-Service store which was crammed with shoppers, jostling one another, their baskets laden, he looked around, a little bewildered. This was foreign country to him. He forced his way to a counter and asked one of the sales girls, 'Where's Friendly . . . your dick?'

'I wouldn't know,' the girl said indifferently. 'Taking a nap, I guess.' She pointed a red fingernail across the store. 'Door marked private . . . if he isn't there, then search me.'

Lepski leered at her.

'Some other time, baby,' he said. 'It would be an interesting experience.'

He left the girl giggling and made his way across the store, pushing and shoving through the milling crowd. He bumped into a tall, thin man with a glass eye and a scar running down his face.

'Can't you look where you're going?' Lepski snarled in his cop voice.

'Pardon me,' the tall man said, side-stepped and continued on towards the exit.

Lepski found the door marked 'Private', pushed it open and walked into a big store room.

Tom Friendly sat on a wooden crate, his fat back against the wall. There was a black hole in the centre of his forehead. His eyes were closed. When Lepski touched him, his big bulky body sagged and rolled slowly to the floor.

Lu-Lu Dodge was picked up by Detective 3rd Grade Sims as she was discussing terms with an elderly man who was trying to make up his mind whether to go with her or not. They were sitting together at the far end of the *Night and Day* bar where Lu-Lu, more often than not, practised her trade.

Sims had been told where to find her by the patrolman on the beat.

'Lu-Lu? Sure . . . The Night and Day. If she isn't in bed, she'll be there.'

Sims, husky and solid, walked into the bar.

As soon as Lu-Lu saw him, she said to her prospective client, 'Fade, honey . . . the cops.'

The elderly man got off his stool and practically ran out of the bar. Sims stood aside and let him go. He moved up to Lu-Lu.

'Come on, baby, we want you,' he said.

'So does every sucker in this goddam city, but it doesn't mean he can have me,' Lu-Lu said. 'So what's it all about?'

'Remember those two guys who picked up Nona Jacey when she left the Pen?' Sims said. 'We want to find them. You could help. It just means looking at some photographs. You play with us and we'll play with you. Look on it as a long-term investment.'

'I bet. That's a laugh,' Lu-Lu said. She finished her drink, thought, then slid off the stool with a show of her legs. 'I liked that kid. Okay. Those two creeps weren't on the force, were they?'

'I wouldn't know,' Sims said, walking with her to the exit. 'I'm never told a thing.'

'That I can understand,' Lu-Lu said, getting into the waiting police car. 'It's a wonder to me you know you're alive.'

They arrived outside Police Headquarters as the City Hall clock was striking the half hour.

Keegan was sitting in the Thunderbird, parked across the road. He waited until Lu-Lu began to walk up the broad stone steps, then he lifted his silenced .38 and shot her neatly and professionally through the back of her head.

Alice Sims had been the chambermaid at the Belvedere Hotel for the past thirty years. She was a gaunt, tall woman, now seventy-three years of age and was considered by the hotel management as a shining example of what a chambermaid should be.

She was in charge of the two most expensive and most luxurious suites in the hotel. She and Josh, the Negro valet, cleaned and serviced the suites, looked after the occupants, saw there were always fresh flowers and they did their work with the least inconvenience to the pampered occupants.

Alice Sims cleaned the main sitting-rooms and the bathrooms at six o'clock in the morning and again at eight o'clock in the evening. It was understood that at those hours the occupants were either in bed or would be out.

She let herself into Mervin Warren's suite a few minutes before six o'clock and began her work. Her methodical method of dusting had been overlooked by Lindsey. Alice Sims had a fetish about dust. Every article in the room received attention from her duster. She even made a habit of dusting under the tables. It was while she was on hands and knees, chasing dust, feeling her thin old bones creaking as she knelt, that she came upon the microphone stuck to the under-panel of the big table.

Although seventy-three years of age, Alice Sims was a rabid follower of Spy thrillers on the television. She guessed immediately that this black button clamped to the table was a microphone and she examined it curiously. It was now common knowledge in the hotel that Mervin Warren, head of Rocket Research, was occupying the suite and it didn't take her more than a few doubtful moments to realize that the suite was bugged. Whether on Warren's authority or not, she had no idea, but if not, then she would have to do something about it.

She decided to consult Rube Henkel, the house detective. She was hesitating whether to find him now or whether she should continue with her work when the bedroom door opened and Warren came out, tying the cord of his dressing-gown.

'Good morning, Alice,' Warren said. 'Don't worry about me. I'll go out on the terrace. I can't sleep. Could I bother you for some coffee . . . then you carry on.'

'Yes, sir,' Alice said. She watched Warren walk out on to the terrace, then she hurried to the Service-room where coffee was always ready. She took a prepared tray, poured coffee into a silver coffee pot and returned to the suite. She went out on to the terrace and put the tray on the table. Warren was yawning and staring out across the bay.

'That's fine, Alice,' he said. 'Thank you . . . how quick you've been.'

Alice hesitated, then said in her prim voice, 'Excuse me, sir. It's not my business, of course, but do you know about the microphone under your table?'

Warren was about to pour out the coffee. He nearly dropped the coffee pot as he started around in his chair to stare at her.

'Microphone?'

'Yes, sir. One of the adhesive kind.' No one could tell Alice anything about the modern methods of bugging. 'Under your table, sir.'

Warren got to his feet.

'Show me,' he said, his voice hard and curt.

She led him to the table. Both of them went down on their hands and knees and she pointed out the black button.

Warren also knew everything about bugging. One look at the button told him she wasn't mistaken. He got to his feet.

'All right, Alice, you run along. Never mind about cleaning up,' he said, wondering who was listening to the conversation. He knew the microphone was so sensitive that even their conversation on the terrace had either been recorded or listened to.

Seeing the angry, worried light in his eyes, Alice started for the door.

'Oh, Alice . . .'

She paused.

'Yes, sir?'

'Say nothing to anyone about this. I'm relying on you.'

'I understand, sir,' and she left.

Warren went into the bathroom, turned on the shower and put through a telephone call to Jesse Hamilton. With the sound of the running shower covering his voice, he told Hamilton about the microphone.

'I'll be right over, sir,' Hamilton said. 'Would you ask if you can be moved to another suite? I don't want to disturb the bug and we can't talk where you are. We could trace the receiver. I'll be over in half an hour.'

Jonathan Lindsey also slept badly. He heard the conversation between Warren and Alice Sims. He knew he had to act quickly. He had to get rid of the tape recorder and the receiver. He woke up Fritz Kurt, Radnitz's secretary, a thin, swarthy man who Radnitz had left at the penthouse suite to handle his business while he was away. While Kurt was dressing hurriedly, Lindsey told him the microphone had been discovered.

'Get rid of the recorder. Use the service elevator,' Lindsey said. 'Be careful you're not seen.'

Kurt nodded. He was an excellent man in any emergency. He hurried into the living-room, picked up the heavy recorder and left.

Lindsey grimaced.

He was certainly having little luck, he thought. When he had begun the operation, it seemed fairly simple. Now Warren must know that there was much more behind Forrester's escape than he had been led to believe. Knowing Warren, Lindsey was sure he would guess someone was after the Code. This was something Radnitz had wanted to avoid. Lindsey was also sure that before long the hotel would be crawling with C.I.A. Agents checking every room. He decided to go back to bed. It wouldn't be policy for them to find him awake if or when they did come.

It wasn't until a C.I.A. specialist had tested the big room that the hotel management had put at Warren's disposal on the third floor, making sure there were no bugging devices, that Warren and Hamilton felt free to talk.

Warren said, 'We've got the picture now, Jesse. This is a conspiracy to get Forrester's formula. Could be either Russia or China. We've lost Forrester. Every witness who might have given us a lead to him has been wiped out. Someone vicious and ruthless is behind all this. We must find him!'

'What's more important, sir . . . we have to find Forrester,' Hamilton said quietly. 'That bug is a powerful one. I thought at first someone in the hotel could be listening in, but with its range, anyone in a car with a recorder could have picked up our talk within half a mile. We'll be wasting time trying to find them. I've already talked to the hotel manager. He says it is out of the question to search every room in the hotel. The people here wouldn't stand for it. They could kick up such a fuss the press will get on to it. No . . . we have got to find Forrester.'

'Any news?'

'Not so far.'

Warren paced the room, then he said, 'I'm leaving for Washington right away. There's nothing more I can do here. This is now up to you and Williams. This is now top level. I must report direct to the President. What I want to assure him is that Forrester can't leave the country.'

Hamilton thrust his chin out.

'I'll guarantee even more than that, sir. He can't leave Florida. Every exit is sealed.'

Warren looked out of the big window at the busy harbour below. Yachts were leaving and coming in. Motorboats off for a day's marlin fishing were roaring out to sea.

'He could be in any of those boats.'

Hamilton shook his head.

'Every boat is being checked before it gets clearance. There is a complete net around Florida. Forrester just can't get out!'

CHAPTER FIVE

ON THE THIRD NIGHT of Paul Forrester's disappearance, Lindsey was served an excellent dinner on the penthouse terrace. He ate without appetite for he had received a coded Telex from Radnitz that read:

I return November 15th. Expect successful results.

Lindsey's alarm reports to Radnitz had been ignored. The Telex told him the ball was firmly in his court. Radnitz was not only leaving him to handle the situation, but expected him to succeed.

Lindsey had refrained from going to the cave hide-out until now. He had no wish to remain long in a series of caves. These caves didn't conform to his high standard of living. He wanted Forrester and Nona Jacey to get settled and also he wanted Dr. Kuntz to have time to make an examination and to come to a conclusion.

A little after ten p.m., Lindsey left the hotel and drove towards the desert. From the newspapers and the radio, he learned that the search for Paul Forrester was being intensified in the City. The helicopter search of the desert had been called off. Police headquarters and the City Hall were being bombarded by reports that Forrester had been seen. Every call had to be checked: so far, every call had proved a false alarm.

Once on the road to the desert, Lindsey took the precaution of turning off his headlights and driving only on his parkers.

He arrived at the entrance to the caves some minutes before ten-thirty. Silk was there to meet him. In the shadows were two men armed with automatic rifles.

As Lindsey got out of the Cadillac, he asked, 'Any trouble?'

'No . . . Kuntz is belly-aching . . . nothing else,' Silk told him.

'The girl?'

'She's okay. I let her have a look at Chet. He scared her pants right off her. She'll do just what she's told.'

'And Forrester?'

Silk fingered the scar on his face, then shrugged.

'I wouldn't know . . . a zombie. You see for yourself.'

The two men walked down the tunnel that led to the first cave.

'I'll talk to Kuntz.' Lindsey looked around. The cave was lit by three big battery-driven lamps. There was a long table, chairs, a radio and against one of the sloping walls a Calor gas cooking range. 'I see you've settled in.'

'It's okay. We eat. Do we stay here long?' Silk was already getting bored living underground in this way.

Lindsey ignored the question. He asked, 'Where's Kuntz?'

'I'll take you to him.'

They walked on to another cave where three men, automatic rifles by their sides, were playing cards. They looked up, then went on playing.

In the next cave, further down the tunnel, Lindsey found Dr. Kuntz sitting in an armchair, reading a medical journal. When he saw Lindsey, he threw down the journal and jumped to his feet.

'How long am I to stay here?' he demanded, his little black eyes flashing. 'This is impossible! Living in a cave! I have repeatedly complained! This man is insolent!'

'All right, doctor,' Lindsey said with his charming smile. 'Please relax.' He waved Silk away and then sat down in a chair and looked around the small cave. 'I wouldn't say this is bad,' he went on, taking a boiled sweet from a tin he carried. He put the sweet into his mouth. 'I would have thought this cave was better—a lot better—than a cell in a German jail. From what I have heard, German jails are to be avoided.' He sucked his sweet, turning it around in his mouth, then as Kuntz slowly sat down, he went on, 'Well now, doctor, how about your patient? What do you make of him?'

Kuntz swallowed down his rage with an obvious effort. He sat silent for several moments, controlling himself, then seeing that Lindsey was watching him, his smile slightly jeering, he forced himself to become professional.

'Frankly, I don't know,' he said. 'I have studied his medical history. Dr. Hertz is one of the leading specialists for mental disorders in the country. He has stated . . .'

'I am not interested in what Dr. Hertz has stated,' Lindsey broke in. 'I'm only interested in your opinion. I know what Hertz has said. I have also studied his report.'

Kuntz shifted uneasily.

'There is nothing really constructive that I can add to his report,' he said. 'For over twenty-six months the patient hasn't responded to any kind of treatment. It is puzzling, but a fact.'

'How about your special operation, doctor?' Lindsey asked, leaning forward.

Kuntz shook his head.

'I'm afraid not. The operation wouldn't be successful. It could even do considerable damage.'

Lindsey's smile faded. This was something he had not expected to hear. He thought of Radnitz. *I return November 15th. Expect successful results.* Failure was out of the question. He knew Radnitz. If he did fail, if Radnitz didn't get his hands on the Soviet's four million dollars, then that would be the end of his association with Radnitz. He knew Radnitz had only to lift a telephone receiver and Silk would appear with his silenced gun. Lindsey felt a sudden cold, creepy sensation run up his spine.

'You will have to do better than that, doctor,' he said, a slight grating note in his voice. 'Just why won't your brilliant operation that has cost so many Jewish lives work with Forrester?'

Kuntz winced.

'For one thing,' he said, not looking at Lindsey, 'I have a strong suspicion that Forrester is not a manic depressive. I've made every possible test on him for the past two days. They are all negative. The operation is only successful when I get positive reactions . . . I'm just not getting them. Therefore, my operation could do far more damage than if he was left alone.'

Lindsey crunched down on his sweet. It was just preventing his mouth from turning dry.

'Are you telling me he is faking?' he demanded.

'Oh, no. Don't get that idea,' Kuntz said 'Let me put it this way. Imagine his mind as a very delicate watch. The hairspring and the balance of the watch are the parts that make the watch keep accurate time. With some people the balance is not entirely adjusted . . . the watch goes either fast or slow. Now with Forrester not only is the balance maladjusted, but through overwork and finding his wife unfaithful, the hairspring also has come out of true. Now it needs only the slightest adjustment to get the balance and the hairspring working properly again. If you had a watch acting like this and you tapped it sharply, it is quite possible the watch would work normally again. You can't of course tap Forrester, but it is possible to give him a mental tap. This tap must come from outside and not from a doctor. It is likely that in a week . . . a month . . . a year or several years something will occur to give him this mental tap and make him normal. But science can't do this. It is far too delicate . . . far too dangerous. The tap could be too strong. If that happened then he will go over the edge and there will be nothing anyone can do for him.'

Lindsey drew in a long breath.

"A week . . . a month . . . years?' he said.

'Yes, but it could happen tomorrow. It depends. It might not happen for years. He has been in this state now for twenty-six months. So far nothing has had any effect on him.'

'Why do you think that?'

Kuntz shrugged his fat shoulders.

'I would say it is because he has been isolated. He has been taken out of his environment. He has had no contact with people he has known. He has had no chance at all of receiving this mental tap I'm talking about.'

Lindsey suddenly realized how clever Radnitz was. It humiliated him to realize that Radnitz was one step ahead of even this brilliant mental specialist and miles ahead of Lindsey's own thinking. He remembered Radnitz saying: *He had a lab assistant, a young woman whose name is Nona Jacey. She is important.*

Now, Lindsey realized why Nona Jacey was so important and why Radnitz had arranged for her to be kidnapped.

For one thing, he has been isolated. He has had no contacts with people he has known. Kuntz had just said.

Radnitz had anticipated this thinking. This was the reason why the girl was here.

Lindsey thought for a long moment, then he said, 'We have here, doctor, Forrester's lab assistant who worked with him before his breakdown. Could she be a possible contact to put him back on balance?'

Kuntz's little eyes narrowed. He stroked his beaky nose, then he shrugged.

"I don't know. It is possible.'

Lindsey decided that Kuntz didn't appreciate the seriousness of the situation. It was time to throw a scare into this fat little man.

'If we fail in this operation,' he said quietly, 'I could not guarantee your safety. I want you to understand that. I doubt very much if you would leave this cave.' He forced a smile. 'The matter is far too important for failure. I must ask for your utmost co-operation.' He paused, then went on, 'We have the girl. It is now up to you to tell me how I should use her to have the maximum effect. Should we fail . . . well, let us not stress the point. We mustn't fail.'

'I don't understand,' Kuntz said, his face paling. 'Leave this cave? You . . .'

'Look, doctor, I've said we won't stress the point. You either bring this man back to normal or our friend with the glass eye wipes you out.' Lindsey got to his feet. 'You have been in constant touch with people who have had to die. Be careful that this isn't your turn.'

Kuntz sat in a cold fat heap, staring up at him.

'I—I will do my best,' he said, his voice quavering.

'Of course,' Lindsey said. He took another sweet from the tin. 'You had better see the girl and talk to her. I understand she is ready to co-operate.'

He watched Kuntz heave himself out of his chair and walk unsteadily from the cave and down the passage and out of sight.

Nona Jacey was terrified.

The previous day a blond, baby-faced man had come quietly into the small cave where she was sitting on the camp bed and had smiled at her. There was something about him that sent a chill of fear through her. He had sat on the bed by her side. He talked in a soft, drawling voice and he told her what would happen to her if she wasn't co-operative. What he told her revolted and horrified her. She put her hands over her ears. This was a mistake. He caught her wrists and flattened her face down on the bed. He leaned on her and continued to talk. The heat of his body and the filth of his words shattered her.

When he had left her sobbing and shuddering on the bed, Sheila came to her. She didn't touch her, but sat by her side, watching her.

'It's all right, honey,' she kept saying. 'He won't do anything . . . you just must do what they tell you. I swear he won't do anything to you.'

Then the following night, this night, a fat beady-eyed man had come in. He had talked to her, asking questions about her association with Forrester. She could see he was as frightened as she was. She answered all his questions truthfully. She was shivering and her hands were shaking. The fat, beady-eyed man kept looking at her hands until to hide them, she sat on them.

He went away.

Sheila had stayed in the shadows, sitting on an upright chair and when the fat, beady-eyed man had gone, she had come over to Nona and had put her arm around her.

'It's all right, honey . . .' she began, but Nona shook her off, screaming in an hysterical voice. 'Get away from me!'

'Sure, sure, sure, honey, I know just how you feel,' Sheila said and looking at her, Nona saw with horror that the girl was twitching, her nose was contracting and as white as wax and there were sweat beads on her face. Sheila saw her look of horror and she grimaced.

'Don't worry about me, honey. I—I just want a fix. That bastard holds it over me. He has let me go until I'm blowing my top. But, you don't have to worry about me. I'll get it. He'll give it to me,' and she left the cave at a stumbling run.

Completely demoralized, terrified and shaken, Nona crouched on the bed, her face in her hands. Then she heard a quiet, cultured voice saying, 'I'm afraid you are having a bad time, Miss Jacey.'

She started and looked up. The tall, white-haired man, immaculately dressed, was regarding her with sympathetic blue eyes. Nona stared at him and caught her breath in a sobbing gasp.

Lindsey looked around for a chair, pulled one up close to her and sat down.

'I'm sorry about all this, Miss Jacey. I assure you you have nothing to be frightened about. May I explain?'

His quiet, charming smile made an immediate, soothing impact on Nona. She dabbed her eyes with her handkerchief and managed to sit upright. She looked questioningly at him.

'Who—who are you?' she asked, her voice unsteady.

'You must look on me as a friend,' Lindsey said, crossing his long legs. He took from his pocket his tin of sweets. 'Do you like sweets? I'm a bit of an addict. Do have one.'

She shuddered away from the tin of highly coloured boiled sweets, shaking her head.

'You don't have to be so frightened,' Lindsey said, taking an orange coloured sweet from the tin. He examined it critically before putting it into his mouth. 'I am very sorry about all this. You will understand just why you are here when I have explained.' He turned the sweet in his mouth. 'Some time ago, you worked for Dr. Paul Forrester. As you know, Dr. Forrester is suffering from a strange mental disease. It is essential that he should be brought back to normal. He has invented a metal.

You know all about that. The formula for making this metal is in code and the code is unbreakable. You also know about this. Dr. Forrester is the only person who can break this code. You happen to be in the position to bring him back to normal so that he can decode his formula.' He paused to smile at her. 'Are you following me?'

Nona was listening. She nodded.

'Good. The urgency to break the code is why all these disagreeable things have been happening to you,' Lindsey went on. 'You are here to help bring Dr. Forrester back to normal. A mental specialist tells me that Forrester needs a past contact. He should unexpectedly meet someone he has known well. This contact could re-adjust him. So what you will have to do is not very difficult. But first, I want to know if you will help him re-adjust.'

Nona's mind was now alive. She realized this man could not be working for the American Government. From the long interrogation she had had to face from the C.I.A. and the F.B.I. she had long ago known the vital importance of Forrester's invention. She now realized this man, with his smooth manners and his charming smile, must be working for a foreign power . . . probably Russia.

'I don't think I can help,' she said, forcing her voice to sound firm. 'Dr. Forrester's invention belongs to America.'

Lindsey smiled.

'My dear young lady, no one is talking about Dr. Forrester's invention. I am asking you to help him get re-adjusted.'

'I can't help,' Nona said.

Lindsey raised his right foot and regarded his glossy toe-cap. He sucked his sweet, then he looked at her, his smile kindly.

'In your present position, Miss Jacey, you really have no alternative but to co-operate.' There was no threat in his smile. His blue eyes were even a little sad. 'This emergency is far too important for you even to think of being unco-operative. What you will be asked to do is very simple. You will see Dr. Forrester and talk to him as you used to talk to him. There will be a microphone and I will be listening to your conversation. I mention this in case you might imagine you can say what you like and not what you will have been told to say. It is hoped that a contact with you could put Dr. Forrester on balance. It is a theory . . . nothing more than that, but it might work.' He got to his feet. 'I will leave you to think it over. If you find you can't co-operate . . .' He paused and crunched down on his sweet, then he lifted his shoulders. 'You have already met Keegan. In my opinion he is a disgusting and revolting animal. I am sure you share my opinion. If you feel you can't co-operate, then there is no point in my staying in these dreary caves. If I leave, you will have no protection. Think about all this seriously, Miss Jacey,' and again smiling, Lindsey walked out of the cave.

She was left alone for over an hour. This was a psychological mistake on Lindsey's part. He had imagined that leaving her with this threat of Keegan hanging over her, he would completely break her, but he had misjudged her. The time lapse gave her time to think, to understand her position and to stiffen her morale.

When Sheila Latimer eventually came into the cave, her eyes glittering, her expression relaxed, Nona had decided what she had to do. She had decided if she were able to help Forrester re-adjust, she must do it. It would then be up to him to give these people the formula or not. Somehow, she must warn him what was going on and that he was more likely than not in the hands of Russian agents.

Sheila, carrying a white overall, said, 'Hi, honey . . . I got my fix. Man! Was I crawling up a wall! You all set for your act?'

'Yes, I'm all set,' Nona said and got to her feet.

'Oh, honey, I'm so glad,' Sheila said. 'They think you should wear this.' She held up the overall. 'I found it with your things. Put it on, sweetheart,' and as Nona slipped into the overall, Sheila stood back and admired her. 'You don't know how sweet you look in that thing. Like a nurse . . . Florence Nightingale. Oh, honey . . . you look divine.'

Dr. Kuntz came into the cave. At the sight of him, Sheila stopped gushing.

'I'll leave you, honey. You've nothing to worry about. Just do what the doc tells you. Honest honey, you've really nothing to worry about,' and waving her hands and side-stepping Kuntz she left the cave.

The fat little doctor sat on the edge of a chair, waving Nona to sit on the bed.

'You are about to take part in a very delicate experiment,' he said as she sat down. 'You are going to meet my patient after a period of some twenty-eight months.' Dr. Kuntz paused, looking at Nona who sat motionless, her pale face expressionless. 'You must be completely natural with him. If by chance the sight of you puts him back on balance, it is possible he won't remember being in the sanatorium . . . it is even possible that he will believe that today is twenty-eight months ago. Do you understand?'

Nona nodded.

'A lot depends on how you handle the situation. It is a big responsibility. Once you come face to face with him, you will have to talk and act according to his reactions. You mustn't contradict anything he says. This is important. Since he has been in the sanatorium, he has acted like a zombie. If, by seeing you, you jolt his mind alive, you must be very careful how you behave. This is your responsibility. We will be listening to your conversation, but we can't help you. Here is what you tell him . . .'

The beady-eyed doctor talked on and on, his fat hands moving expressively as he talked while Nona, her chin in her hands, listened.

The first tiny crack in the wall of security that Jonathan Lindsey had constructed to keep the Forrester operation secret came when Chief of Police Terrell parked outside his bungalow, ten minutes past midnight.

He felt discouraged. So far there was no lead and Forrester had completely vanished. Troops, police and Federal Agents were even at this late hour still searching every likely hiding place in the city.

Terrell had been at his desk for thirty-eight continuous hours. Beigler had relieved him, and now all he was thinking of as he got out of his car was his comfortable bed and sleep.

He heard a horn tap . . . a single note, and pausing at his gate, he looked over his shoulder. A black Buick Wildcat was parked across the street. A man sat at the wheel, a cigarette between his lips and as Terrell looked at him, the man waved.

Terrell never carried a gun. He was Chief of Police and believed in his authority. He was completely fearless and walking slowly, without hesitation, he crossed to the car. He recognized the man behind the driving wheel. It was Shane O'Brien who Terrell knew ran the Go-Go Club on the Eastside waterfront.

Terrell came to rest by the car.

'You wanted me?'

'Evening, Chief,' O'Brien didn't look at Terrell but stared through the windshield down the badly lit road, his eyes watchful. 'Could we take a little ride? This street isn't healthy for me.'

Terrell knew immediately that O'Brien had information for

him. He was surprised. Up to now, O'Brien had run his Club well, kept clear of the police and clear of trouble. He was the last man Terrell would expect to turn informer.

Terrell got in beside O'Brien who set the car moving. He drove around the back streets, then slowed and pulled up by a vacant lot.

'I read about Drena French,' he said, lighting a cigarette. 'She wasn't drunk. She didn't fall into the wet. She was knocked off. I don't know why, but I think I know who did it. I can't prove it and I don't want to prove it. I'm risking my neck and my Club talking this way, but I liked the girl.'

Terrell sucked at his unlit pipe. He didn't say anything. He waited.

'A guy came to the Club the night before she kicked off,' O'Brien went on. 'He said he wanted to talk to Drena. I know him. He's dangerous. I warned Drena, but they talked together, then she came to me and asked if she could leave. This guy had a business proposition for her. He had already given her three-hundred bucks to get her interested. I told her to watch out. She left with him. The next night she was telling Tin-Tin she was going to buy The Seagull Restaurant. I think this guy must have offered her a big lump of money and double-crossed her. I think he was the one who knocked her off.'

'Tell me about him,' Terrell said, no longer sleepy. He was sitting upright, looking at O'Brien's lean profile.

'His name is Chet Keegan,' O'Brien said. 'He works with a guy called Lu Silk. They are deadly poison. I don't know anything else about them. They always seem to have plenty of money . . . always well dressed. They're not hooked up with the gangs around here. They work on their own, but they have a reputation of being dynamite.' He looked sharply at Terrell. 'This is a tip, Chief. This has to be strictly under the wraps. I'm tipping you because I liked the girl.'

Terrell sighed.

'Okay, O'Brien. Anything else?'

'No.' O'Brien started the car. 'I'll take you home.'

They drove in silence until they reached Terrell's bungalow. Then O'Brien said, 'I hope you nail those two bastards.'

Terrell got out of the car.

'So long,' he said and walked over to his car. O'Brien drove rapidly away. Terrell hesitated. He longed for his bed, but now there was work to do. He got in his car and lifted the telephone receiver that gave him direct contact with Beigler's desk.

Beigler said: 'Sergeant's desk . . . City Police.'

'Listen, Joe,' Terrell said. 'I want everything that you can dig up about two men: Chet Keegan and Lu Silk. This is top priority. I'm now going to bed. I'll be at headquarters at eight o'clock. I want the dope right there on my desk.'

'Nothing but names?' Beigler asked.

'Nothing but names,' Terrell returned and hung up.

Wearily he got out of the car, locked the doors, then plodded up the garden path to his front door. He saw with relief there was a light on in the sitting-room. Carrie was waiting up for him.

At headquarters, Beigler replaced the telephone receiver, drank some coffee and lit a cigarette. While he was doing this, his brain was in top gear. There was one man he was sure could give him quick information about these two the Chief was interested in. A man named Carl Hegger who was Beigler's own stool pigeon: a man who knew everything there was to know about the underworld.

Beigler looked at Lepski who was reading the comic strips, yawning and mussing his hair and every now and then looking at his watch. In ten minutes he would be off duty and going back to his wife. Since he and Carroll had only been married for two months, the return to his marriage bed was something he looked forward to with relish.

'Tom,' Beigler said, getting to his feet. 'You're promoted. Take over the desk. I have outside business,' and before Lepski could scream a protest, Beigler was gone.

Beigler drove fast to Hegger's apartment. Leaving the car, he took the shaky elevator to the third floor and rang the doorbell. As he waited, he looked at his strap watch. The time was twenty-five minutes to one.

The door opened and Hegger stood in the doorway: a short, heavily built man, balding with a broad fleshy face and deepset black eyes. He was wearing a pair of bottle green pyjamas and his hair was mussed. He looked as if he had just got out of bed.

'You alone?' Beigler asked, pushing his way into the small but tidy sitting-room.

'Me and the cat,' Hegger said. 'What a time to call! What's up?'

'Has the cat got two or four legs?' Beigler demanded, knowing Hegger's weakness for blondes.

Hegger hesitated and then shrugged.

'Okay . . . if it's business, let's go for a little ride.' He looked uneasily at his bedroom door. 'I've just got this cat thawed out . . .

she's been an iceberg for weeks. Let's hurry it up. She could freeze up again.'

'I'll wait down on the street,' Beigler said and left the apartment.

Ten minutes later, he and Hegger were driving around the block. Beigler was asking questions.

'Poison,' Hegger said when he heard the names. 'Don't kid yourself for one second . . . they are sheer poison. They have plenty of protection. I could give you a breakdown on them, but what's it worth?'

'I'll spring twenty bucks,' Beigler said.

Hegger sniggered.

'Let me out. I'll walk back. The exercise will do me good.'

Beigler pulled up. He turned and tapped Hegger on his fat chest.

'I said twenty bucks.' His voice was cop hard. 'If you don't put up, buster, I'll take you in right now. I'm not fooling. This is important. I'll throw you to Olsen. Have you forgotten that you laid his daughter some months ago? He doesn't know, but I could tell him.'

Hegger flinched.

'It wasn't my fault,' he said feverishly. 'She practically raped me!'

'You tell Olsen that . . . he'll love it.' Beigler took two ten dollar bills from his wallet. 'Now talk.'

Hegger took the money and stowed it away in his pocket.

'These two are pros. They murder for money. Keegan was a pimp. Silk is the real dangerous one. They have an apartment on Belleview Avenue . . . No. 196, top floor. They're working for someone who pays big money. There's a whisper that the guy's name is Jonathan Lindsey. I wouldn't swear to it, but the whisper came from the right direction.'

'Know anything about Jonathan Lindsey?' Beigler asked.

Hegger shook his head.

'Not a thing . . . I just heard the name mentioned.'

'Keep going. What else?'

'Nothing else. When I hear guys are poison, I keep my nose out of their business. I like to remain strong and healthy. That's the lot, sergeant. Nothing else.'

From past experience when dealing with Hegger, Beigler knew there was nothing more he could get out of him, but at least, he had a name: something to move the investigation forward.

'Not much for my money,' he said as he drove Hegger back to his apartment.

'Wait and see,' Hegger said with a sly grin. 'I've never cheated you yet, have I?'

As he got out of the car, Beigler said, 'Mind that cat doesn't scratch you.'

'I like being scratched,' Hegger returned and crossed the sidewalk to his front door as fast as his short legs could carry him.

Nona Jacey stood at the entrance to the L-shaped cave that was lit by four powerful electric lamps high in the roof. Dr. Kuntz and Lindsey stood by her side.

'Go ahead, Miss Jacey,' Lindsey said. 'Don't be nervous. We are right here. Just do what you have been told, and don't forget we are listening to what is being said.'

Nona braced herself, then urged on by a slight push by Dr. Kuntz's hot, fat hand, she walked into the cave.

The size of the cave surprised her. It was the last of the series and seemed to her to be immense. At the far end of the cave, as she turned the corner, she could see a bed, a table, four upright chairs and a lounging chair. As she walked slowly forward, her shadow became long and thin, advancing before her.

Paul Forrester was sitting in the lounging chair. She was frightened of this man who was sitting so still. She had heard the behind-the-hand gossip about him. There had been rumours that he had caught Jack Leadbeater, his Chief Assistant, in bed with that awful wife of his and had killed him savagely with a knife. The rumours also said that five men had been needed to subdue him as they came on him, battering down the bathroom door where his wife was cowering and screaming.

Dr. Kuntz had explained Forrester's condition to her. She knew she was approaching a man who could suddenly turn violent. Although she knew Dr. Kuntz and Lindsey were just out of sight, she wondered a little fearfully if they could reach her in time should Forrester attack her.

Forrester sat in the full light. His long legs were crossed, his hands rested in his lap. His black hair now had a few streaks of white at the temples and his face was thinner, otherwise he still looked as she had last seen him when he left for Washington some twenty-nine months ago. He was a distinguished looking man in his late thirties with blunt features, heavy black eyebrows and a cleft chin: a man she had always admired for his patience, his kindness and his tremendous enthusiasm for work.

She paused within ten feet of him and looked steadily at him, aware her heart was pounding.

He peered at her. His face was expressionless; his eyes blank.

'Dr. Forrester . . . it's Nona,' she said.

Again he peered at her. Then suddenly his eyes became alive.

'Nona . . . is it really you?'

'Yes.'

He smiled, then got to his feet.

'What are you doing here?' he asked. 'I'm glad to see you . . . at last, a friendly face. I seem to be living in a nightmare.' He looked around. 'This cave . . . how did I get here? Do you know where we are?'

Nona realized from what she had been told by Dr. Kuntz that the sight of her had put Forrester back on balance. She couldn't quite believe it, but his sudden animation reduced her feeling of fear.

'You have been seriously ill, Dr. Forrester,' she said unsteadily. She was saying what Kuntz had told her to say. 'Mr. Warren has moved us here. It is for security reasons.'

'It's a cave, isn't it? How extraordinary,' Forrester said. 'But sit down. Tell me about it, Nona. Warren has put us here?'

Nona sat on the edge of one of the upright chairs. Forrester resumed his seat, looking curiously at her.

'Yes,' Nona said. 'Don't you remember? You were taken ill. You—You had a blackout. Mr. Warren wants you to continue to work on the formula. That's why we are here.'

Forrester frowned. He rubbed his forehead.

'Formula . . . what formula?' he asked finally.

'Formula ZCX,' Nona said, watching him.

'Oh, that.' He regarded her, his eyebrows lifting. 'Did you tell Warren about that?' There was a hint of reproach in his voice.

'I had to . . . you have been seriously ill. You perhaps don't understand. You've been ill for some time. They kept asking me questions . . . I had to tell them.'

She knew this was not what Dr. Kuntz had told her to say, but he had given her a free hand. Both he and Lindsey had told her she must play the cards as they came to her.

'So Warren knows about the formula.' Forrester's face became suddenly remote. 'He has it?'

'Yes.'

'Well, then why should they worry me about it? If he has it, then let someone else handle it.'

'But they can't break the code, Dr. Forrester,' Nona said in a small voice.

Forrester smiled.

'No . . . I don't suppose they can. You know, Nona, I'm not interested any more in formulas . . . ideas . . . codes . . . they bore me. I'm quite happy to remain as I am. Have you seen Thea recently? Has she inquired after me?'

Listening to all this, Lindsey looked inquiringly at Dr. Kuntz who nodded. Leaning close to Lindsey, he whispered, 'I believe it has worked. He is talking rationally . . . something he hasn't done before. We will have to rebrief the girl. Shall I go in?'

Lindsey hesitated, then nodded.

'All right. I leave it to you.'

Dr. Kuntz moved forward, turned the corner of the cave as Nona was saying, 'I don't know, Dr. Forrester. I haven't seen her.'

Forrester said, 'Do you know where she is? I would . . .' He paused as he saw Dr. Kuntz coming towards him. His face immediately became a blank mask. It was as if a shutter had fallen behind his eyes.

Dr. Kuntz forced a genial smile on his fat face.

'You may remember me, Dr. Forrester. I am Dr. Kuntz. I have been looking after you. I am glad to see you are making such a splendid recovery.'

The blank, cold eyes showed no sign of hearing what Kuntz was saying. Forrester was back in his zombie state.

Kuntz signalled to Nona to leave. She got to her feet, looked at the still figure that had lost all animation, her heart pounding, then she walked unsteadily out of the cave.

Lindsey had been watching all this. He smiled at her as she approached him.

'A very good try, Miss Jacey,' he said. 'You got through to him. Let's go back to your room—if I may call it that—and we'll discuss the next move.'

He walked with her along the dimly lit tunnel back to the small cave. He sat down and waved her to sit on the bed. He took a folded newspaper from his pocket, shook it open and handed it to her.

'Did you see he did this?' he asked quietly. 'He killed his nurse. I want you to tell him tomorrow what he has done and to show him this newspaper. It is important now for him to realize he has reached the point of no return. He must either work with us, Miss Jacey, or he will go back to the sanatorium for good. We can get him out of the country in a little while. There could be a big future for him in Moscow. They treat men like Dr. Forrester very well.'

Nona was scarcely listening. She was reading with horror of

Fred Lewis's murder. Then abruptly, she looked at Lindsey, her eyes flashing.

'I don't believe it! I'm sure Dr. Forrester . . .'

Lindsey raised his hand, shaking his head at her.

'It's not what you believe, Miss Jacey, but what the police and public opinion believe that counts,' he said. 'Now, listen carefully to what I have to say.'

Captain Terrell breezed into his office just after eight a.m. He was a man who needed very little sleep. He had had six hours of dreamless rest, a big breakfast and he was raring to go. Not so Joe Beigler. As soon as he heard Terrell enter his office, he got wearily to his feet and left the Detectives' room.

Lepski who was still coping with the routine work, called after him: 'Ask him if his bed was nice and comfy, Joe.' His voice was loaded with sarcasm. Beigler ignored him. He tapped on Terrell's door, then entered the small office.

Terrell regarded him sympathetically.

'Had a rough night, Joe?' he asked, waving to a chair.

'Rough enough, Chief. You want some coffee?'

'Not right now. Sit down. What's cooking?'

Beigler lowered his bulk onto the hard upright chair. He told Terrell what he had learned from Carl Hegger.

'That didn't get me far, but a tip is a tip,' he went on. 'I checked on this guy Hegger mentioned: Jonathan Lindsey. I couldn't find him in the telephone book so I called the big hotels. I found him at the Belvedere. He was occupying the most expensive suite in the hotel until yesterday morning. The suite is on a yearly rental to a guy called Herman Radnitz. He's away and Lindsey is expected back any time.'

'Who is Radnitz?' Terrell asked, picking up a pencil and beginning to make notes.

'Yeah . . . that's a question,' Beigler said. 'I went around to the hotel. I was lucky to catch Rube Henkel, the hotel dick.' Beigler paused to light a cigarette, then he shook his head. 'We'll have to watch our step here, Chief. The hotel and Henkel look on Radnitz and Lindsey as sacred. I mean just that. I didn't press it. When I asked Henkel what he thought about Lindsey, he nearly flipped his lid.' Beigler took out his notebook and opened it. 'When I asked him who Radnitz was, he . . . well, here's what he said, Chief,' and reading from the notebook, he went on, 'We have known Mr. Radnitz and Mr. Lindsey for years. They are very V.I.P. We consider them to be our best clients. Have you gone screwy or something? Look, sergeant, we don't talk about people like them. They are top ranking. Just what is all this about?' Beigler shut his notebook. 'I got the idea if I didn't pour out the oil, Henkel would go running to Radnitz and Lindsey and start flapping with his mouth. I didn't think you would want that, so I cooked a quickie about a hit and run case and we thought it might be Lindsey. I said the car involved was a 1961 Chevvy. Henkel said I must be out of my mind and that Lindsey drove a Caddy. He gave me a description of Lindsey. It's down in my report. I apologized, ate dirt and we parted friends.

'And Radnitz?' Terrell asked.

'I got Hamilton out of bed.' There was a grin of satisfaction on Beigler's face. 'I thought he might do some work. He said he would check with Washington and he would be around here as soon as he had got some dope.'

'And these other two: Keegan and Silk?'

'I've given them to Williams. I got him out of bed too. His men are better at this than we are. He has two men watching Silk's place. Williams and I decided not to push it, but the apartment is sewn up tight.'

Terrell nodded approvingly.

'You've done a good job, Joe. Now get off. I'll take over. It's time you caught up with some sleep.'

'I'll stick,' Beigler said. 'This is getting interesting. I don't want to miss anything.'

'You won't. You get off and take Lepski with you. You're no use to me without some sleep. Go on, Joe. If something breaks, I'll call you.'

Twenty minutes after Beigler and Lepski had left headquarters, Hamilton of the C.I.A. and Williams of the F.B.I. arrived. They sat down around Terrell's desk.

'The picture is coming into focus,' Hamilton said. 'I'm leaving for Washington in a couple of hours. You've done a swell job, Chief. We now know Keegan and Silk are hooked up with Lindsey. Lindsey is hooked up with Radnitz. But Radnitz is big. I have his dossier here which I'll leave with you. I'm willing to bet he has Forrester's coded formula. I'll tell you for why. Warren was in Berlin three weeks ago. He had with him his P.S.: Alan Craig. Radnitz was also in Berlin. I've been on to Berlin and have checked all this out.Warren and Craig returned to Washington. Craig is supposed to have committed suicide. A sex photo of him and a queer left in his apartment pointed to the reason for his suicide. The photo was taken in his Paris apartment. I got our man in Paris to check. The queer was found shot to death. From all this, it is a good guess that Craig who had access to Forrester's formula, was blackmailed into giving a copy to Radnitz, then he was murdered. Radnitz always stays at the George V Hotel. The concierge of the hotel remembers that Craig visited Radnitz. Put the bits together and we get the picture, but there is no real proof. This is our pigeon now, Chief. Washington will have to make up its mind how I'm to play it. Radnitz is much too big to push around, but if we can pick up Lindsey or Silk or Keegan, we might be able to push them around.'

Williams said, 'I have two men staked outside Silk and Keegan's place. Suppose we move in, bring them down here and work them over?'

Terrell shook his head.

'Not from what I've heard about them. They're too tough. We would be showing our hands. Let's tail them: stick with them. They could lead us to Forrester.'

Williams hesitated, then nodded.

'I'll have to get more men on the job. We don't even know if they are using the apartment now.'

When he had gone, Hamilton shifted back in his chair and began to load a well used pipe.

'I'll be back tomorrow,' he said. 'I'm pretty certain we can't touch Radnitz. He has too many friends in the right places. But Lindsey . . . we might get at him.'

Terrell lifted his heavy shoulders.

'Give me proof,' he said quietly, 'and I'll arrest the President himself. Big names mean nothing to me. All I want is proof.'

As Hamilton got to his feet, he smiled wryly.

'I'm sure, but Washington doesn't work like that.'

It was while he was driving to the airport to catch the plane to Washington that Lindsey was giving Nona her final instructions. She had passed a restless night, but during the night she had made up her mind to be as unco-operative with Lindsey as she dared. Lindsey had warned her that there was a microphone operating in Forrester's cave. Everything she said to him would be heard. But what Lindsey didn't know was that Forrester was an expert in the deaf and dumb sign language. In the past, when making tape recordings of the sounds of various instruments to do with friction, he had given his instructions to Nona in sign language. She also had become expert so that they could converse together without spoiling the tape.

Lindsey was saying, 'He had a good night. He has been drugged.

You know what to say. Show him the newspaper, then persuade him to talk to me. You understand?'

Nona nodded.

'All right, then go ahead. I'll be listening.' Lindsey gave her his charming smile. 'There is no time to waste. It is important, Miss Jacey, that you should succeed.'

She took the newspaper and followed Lindsey out of the cave. At the entrance to the L-shaped cave, he touched her arm.

'Go ahead,' he whispered. 'Remember it is certainly more important to you than to me that you succeed.' The threat was there although it was softened by the smile.

She found Forrester sitting in the lounging chair, his legs crossed, his hands in his lap.

She walked straight up to him and put the newspaper across his knees.

'Please look at this,' she said, knowing Lindsey was listening.

Forrester stared up at her, then he smiled.

'Hello, Nona. Sit down. What is this?'

'Please look at it,' she repeated and sat down.

He glanced at the paper, then stiffened slightly as he saw the big photograph of himself spread across the front page. He looked at the smaller photograph of Fred Lewis. He read the glaring headlines:

Dr. Paul Forrester Escapes.

Personal Nurse Bludgeoned to Death.

He continued to read, his face remote, his hands shaking a little making the paper rustle. He read of the intense search for him. He looked at the photographs of the circling helicopters and of the troops jumping down from parked trucks to fan out for a house-to-house search. He read the warning:

Dr. Forrester is believed violent. If you see him, don't attempt to approach him. Telephone Police Headquarters. Paradise City 7777.

Finally, he put the paper down and looked at Nona.

'You have read all this?' he asked.

'Yes.'

'Do you believe it?'

'It is what they think,' she returned, then her fingers sprang into life. They said to him in sign language: 'No, I don't. There is a microphone here. They are listening.'

Forrester's eyes became very alert. He sat for some moments, staring at her, then he smiled and nodded.

'I want to think about all his,' he said. 'Please give me time to think. Please don't speak to me.'

They looked at each other, then they began to talk rapidly to each other in sign language.

'Answer my questions,' Forrester spelt out. 'It's the formula?'

'Yes.'

'The Russians?'

'Yes. They say you will be treated well in Moscow.'

'Have they the formula?'

'They must have.'

'I didn't kill this man. I want you to believe me.'

She nodded.

'I believe you. I never thought you did.'

Aloud, Forrester said, 'I don't understand any of this. I thought you told me Warren sent us here. From this newspaper, I have escaped. I seem to have killed my attendant. I remember nothing.' His fingers spelt out, 'I must talk to whoever is handling this. Don't worry . . . it will be all right.'

Nona said aloud, 'There is someone who can explain all this to you, Dr. Forrester. Will you talk to him?'

'I suppose so . . . yes, but I want you to stay with me.'

'All right. I'll get him.'

She stood up and walked across the sandy floor of the cave, turned the corner and found Lindsey waiting.

'He is ready to talk to you,' she said.

'Yes. I've been listening,' Lindsey said. 'You have done very well.' He felt a twinge of conscience as he looked at her. Radnitz had said there were to be no loose ends. Once she had completed her task, she would have to be handed over to Silk. She would be far too dangerous to be free. 'As he wants you with him, let us go together.'

By now Nona had come to realize the worth of his quiet, charming smile. It sent a shiver down her spine. She went with him back to the cave where Forrester was sitting, waiting.

Lindsey took the chair opposite Forrester. Nona moved into the shadows and sat on another chair, away from them.

'I am acting on behalf of the Russian Government,' Lindsey said to Forrester. 'They want your formula. You have had a mental breakdown. Unfortunately, during this breakdown, you killed your Chief Assistant and also your male nurse. You escaped from the sanatorium in which you have been for the past twenty-eight months. You escaped by hitting your nurse with such violence you killed him. By sheer coincidence one of my operators found you wandering the streets. He brought you here where you are quite safe. The Russian Government will give you every protection. They want your formula. Only you are able to decode it. In return for decoding the formula, we will get you away and you can settle in Moscow where you will be treated very well and live very comfortably. First, Dr. Forrester, you must decode the formula. However, if you don't wish to co-operate, then you will be returned to the sanatorium and you will remain there for the rest of your life . . . not a happy thought. Would you like time to think about this or are you prepared to decode the formula now . . . I have it with me.' Lindsey took from a slim brief-case he had brought with him a photocopy of the formula and offered it to Forrester.

Watching, Nona was thankful to see Forrester's hand was steady as he took the stiff sheet of paper and looked at it. He dropped it on the table.

'Yes, I would need time to think about it,' he said after a long pause.

'I don't want to press you,' Lindsey said smoothly, 'but time is important. Can you decode the formula, Dr. Forrester?'

Forrester reached forward and picked up the photocopy. He began to study it. Nona got the idea that he was deliberately taking his time while he thought. A tense three minutes passed, then he looked at Lindsey who could scarcely conceal his impatience.

'It is possible,' he said, paused and then went on, 'but I am not doing it.'

Lindsey's smile faded.

'I'm afraid you have no choice, Dr. Forrester,' he said, sitting forward.

'No choice? Surely that is an exaggeration. Tell me why I have no choice.'

'If you don't decode the formula,' Lindsey said, a slight rasp in his voice, 'then you will be returned to the sanatorium . . . or should I call it the asylum? You don't want that to happen, do you?'

'But why not?' Forrester asked. 'I've been there a long time. I am very well looked after.' He studied Lindsey's lean set face for a long moment, then went on, 'The mistake you are making is you imagine I want my freedom. I don't. I have arrived at a mental state of complete indifference . . . when all this . . .'

he waved to the photocopy, 'means nothing to me. No threat from you or anyone else could possibly influence me. My life is of no value to me. I don't care if I live or die. You should realize this. I could even prefer to be dead.'

Lindsey stared at him. He felt a sudden cold sweat break out on his hands. He thought of Radnitz and that arrogant message: *I return November 15th. Expect successful results.* He thought of Silk and his silenced gun. Forrester's calm, steady gaze worried him.

'You could be persuaded, Dr. Forrester,' he said.

'You think so? Tell me how,' Forrester said quietly.

Lindsey hesitated. He wondered if he should consult Dr. Kuntz then decided he would have to handle this himself.

'I have two men working for me,' he said. 'They are not entirely human. I could order them to make you decode the formula.' He paused, staring at Forrester. 'Sooner or later, the body and the spirit break. Why should you endure such stupid and unnecessary suffering.'

'No one could break me,' Forrester said. 'That is a stupid and unnecessary threat.'

Lindsey took the tin of sweets from his pocket. He selected a raspberry coloured sweet, stared at it, then put it into his mouth.

'They would begin at first with our little friend here,' he said, nodding to Nona. 'That would be bad for your morale. She has already met the man who would deal with her . . . an animal.'

Nona turned cold, but she remained still, watching Forrester. He turned his head slowly and looked at her, his smile reassuring, then he turned back to Lindsey.

'I'm not going to be dishonest with you,' he said. 'I could say, of course, that I had forgotten how to break the code, but I haven't. I could decode the formula in twenty minutes, but I do not intend to do so. Please listen to my reasons carefully. During the months I have been locked away, I have had plenty of time to think seriously about my invention. It may be difficult for you to understand that inventing something new is a challenge to certain people—like myself. However, once the invention has been invented people like myself must ask themselves if this invention could become a menace. This is the reason why I have told no one about my invention. I wanted first to convince myself that I had invented something not only useful but something that could not threaten the peace of this sick, sad world.' Forrester leaned back in his chair, looking down at his hands. 'I suppose this is the crank in me. I know my invention is worth several millions of dollars, but money never has or ever will interest me. When I was in Washington I was approached by Russian and Chinese agents who offered me any money I cared to name for the formula. I refused. They threatened me as you have threatened me. Still I refused. I have decided that my invention is not for this present age. Later, perhaps, when the world has become more adult, it can be safely used, but not now, and when it is used, it is for every nation, not just one.'

Lindsey drew in a slow breath of exasperation.

'I'm afraid, Dr. Forrester, we can't wait. You will decode the formula or take the consequences. The girl will suffer first, and you will watch her suffer.'

Forrester again looked reassuringly at Nona, then he smiled at Lindsey.

'I don't think so. Would you say, because of my formula, that I am, as I sit here, worth anything from three to five million dollars?'

Lindsey's eyes narrowed. He hesitated, then nodded.

'I suppose so.'

'Yes . . . I think that is a fair estimate. You must understand I am what is called a crank. I have already told you I don't care if I live or die. I trust you are intelligent enough to accept this statement as the truth. I repeat: I don't care if I live or die. So what I am now going to do is to get out of this chair and walk out of this cave and I am taking Miss Jacey with me.'

Lindsey stiffened.

'Look, Dr. Forrester, you have been ill . . .' he began, but when Forrester got to his feet, he called sharply: 'Silk!'

Silk, listening to all this, snatched off his headphones and came silently and quickly to the entrance of the cave. He stood under one of the powerful lights and stared at Forrester with his one gleaming eye. Looking at him, Nona caught her breath. The horror she felt from the ravaged, cruel face went through her like a knife stab.

'You will stay here, Dr. Forrester,' Lindsey said, jumping to his feet. 'I don't want to use force, but I will have to if you won't co-operate. You are not leaving here until you have decoded the formula.'

Forrester regarded Silk who stood guarding the exit of the cave. He studied the evil, vicious face with interest.

'Is this the specimen you are threatening me with?' he asked Lindsey.

'Yes, and there's another who will work on the girl,' Lindsey said. 'I'm sorry about all this, but you are forcing my hand. Now, doctor, please be sensible. Please decode the formula and let us have no more dramatics.'

'Miss Jacey and I are leaving,' Forrester said. 'Do I sound confident? I am confident. Let me tell you why. I have already stressed the point, but I will again repeat it: I am completely indifferent whether I live or die. When I was threatened in Washington, I realized I could be kidnapped and tortured. So I took precautions. Since that time I have always kept by me a capsule of cyanogen. It is in my mouth now. I have only to bite on it and I shall be dead. If you try to stop Miss Jacey and I leaving here, I will bite down on the capsule. Have I made myself clear?'

Silk made a move forward, but Lindsey waved him back. He stared at Forrester who was looking calmly at him.

'I don't believe you,' Lindsey said, his face now pale, his voice uncertain. 'You can't bluff me, Dr. Forrester.'

'It isn't bluff,' Forrester said. 'It is an experiment in psychology. Alive, I am worth three to five million dollars. Dead, I am worth nothing. Listening to you, studying you, I have come to the conclusion that you are very concerned with money. I know you would not hesitate to tear out my nails or to use a hot iron on me, but what you can't do, what you can't even contemplate doing is to lose millions of dollars. I am not going to prove to you that I have the capsule in my mouth. I am leaving, and if you make any attempt to stop me or Miss Jacey, you will have destroyed millions of dollars.'

Lindsey's face turned into a snarling, frightened mask.

'If you leave here, you will be caught, you fool!' he rasped. 'They will put you back into a padded cell! Give me the formula, and I swear I will get you to Moscow where you can start a new and important career! You will be honoured . . . you will be able to continue your experiments.'

Forrester shook his head. He beckoned to Nona.

'Come along, Nona. We're going,' he said.

Silk drew his gun.

'Make a move,' he said, 'and I'll kill her. I'm not kidding. Make just one move . . .'

Nona felt her knees sag. She stood motionless, scarcely breathing, then Forrester said quietly, 'Come along, Nona. There is nothing to be frightened about.'

She looked at Silk and at the gun pointing at her. She looked at Lindsey, his face shiny with sweat, and then she looked at

Forrester, quiet, confident, and smiling at her. She went to him and he took her hand, then they started across the sandy floor of the cave, both looking directly at Silk.

Lindsey said in a strangled voice, 'Let them go!'

Forrester kept on. His grip tightened on Nona's hand. His eye glittering with fury, Silk lowered his gun. Forrester continued on past him and into the long tunnel. They passed the three guards who were still playing cards. The men looked up, gaped, then got to their feet. Forrester continued to walk down the tunnel, ignoring them. Nona kept by his side. She was trembling. She heard Lindsey shout: 'Leave them alone!' Forrester kept on. They went past the small cave where Dr. Kuntz was sitting. He stared, got to his feet, hesitated, then stood motionless.

The Thunderbird was parked at the exit of the tunnel.

Forrester paused beside it.

'Can you drive this, Nona?' he asked.

'Yes,' she said shakily.

'Well then, let's use it.' He got into the passenger's seat. She looked back down the tunnel. She could see Silk watching her. She closed her eyes, struggling to control her jumping nerves, then Forrester said, 'Come along, Nona. There's nothing to be frightened about.'

She opened her eyes, took in a deep breath, then slid under the driving wheel. She turned on the ignition, started the car and drove out of the tunnel into the dazzling bright sunlight.

Silk spun around and glared at Lindsey.

'Do you think you played that number well?' he demanded.

Lindsey wiped his sweating face.

'What else could I do? He's mad! We could get him again, but dead . . .'

'Yeah?' Silk shoved his gun savagely back into his holster. 'They will be picked up in less than an hour. They'll talk. We'll have the cops here like a swarm of bees. I'm getting out!' He turned and began to walk swiftly down the tunnel.

'Wait!' Lindsey shouted, but Silk paid no attention. There were several cars parked in the tunnel. The guards came running up as Silk got into a Buick.

'Get lost!' he shouted to them. 'Get the hell out of here! The lid's off!' Then he sent the car hurtling down the deserted road. Far ahead of him, he could see the disappearing cloud of dust made by the Thunderbird.

Lindsey hesitated as he heard the second car start up, then he went quickly down the tunnel to his Cadillac. Dr. Kuntz joined him. Lindsey motioned him to get in the car, then he drove fast from the tunnel.

'What has happened?' Kuntz asked.

'Shut up!' Lindsey snarled. 'Don't talk to me!'

His smooth polish and charm had gone. His fear and his fury was so obvious that Kuntz's fat face went slack. He relapsed into silence. Lindsey sent the Cadillac roaring down the road. His mind was busy. This was the end of his association with Radnitz, he told himself. Silk was right. Forrester and the girl would be quickly picked up. He would be implicated. Even if Forrester didn't talk, the girl would. His one chance was to get to Mexico City before a search for him could get organized. For years now, he had been siphoning off half his income from Radnitz to a bank in Mexico City. He had no fears for his financial future. His immediate problem was his safest and quickest route to Mexico City. He finally decided to take a fast motorboat to Havana, then pick up an air-taxi to Mexico City. He would have to go back to the hotel for his money. It was a risk to return to the hotel, but he had to have cash if he was to hire a fast boat.

He reached the junction of the desert road and the State Highway and he pulled up.

'Get out,' he said the Kuntz. 'You can hitch a ride from here. Go on . . . get out!'

Kuntz stared at him, his beady eyes opening wide.

'What about my fee?' he demanded. 'You promised me . . .'

Lindsey hit him across his face with a furious backhand blow. 'Get out!'

His eyes watering, his nose beginning to bleed, the fat doctor stumbled out of the car. Lindsey slammed the door shut and drove on to the highway, heading towards the hotel.

As he drove, he talked over the car's telephone to the hotel. He told the hall porter that he had to leave at once for Havana and would he get his clothes packed? Would he also have a fast motorboat waiting for him. The hall porter said everything would be arranged.

As Lindsey cut the connection, he thought thankfully of the power of money. He arrived back at the hotel forty minutes later. The hall porter came from behind his desk.

'The boat is waiting, Mr. Lindsey,' he said. 'Your luggage is down here.'

'Thank you,' Lindsey said. 'I have some papers to take with me.' A fifty dollar bill exchanged hands, then Lindsey took the express elevator to the penthouse suite.

It took him only a few minutes to open the safe and take from it a thick packet of $100 bills. These he stuffed into his hip pocket. He looked around at the luxury of the suite and felt a pang of regret that he would be leaving it for good.

He thought of Radnitz now probably in Hong Kong, probably wondering why he hadn't heard from him. Radnitz had too many people on his payroll to fear the Law. He would always be safe.

Well, let him wonder, Lindsey thought. He left the suite for the last time, slamming the door behind him.

CHAPTER SIX

Chet Keegan was enjoying himself.

He was in the apartment which he shared with Silk. Both the men believed in luxury living. They had had the apartment done over by an expert, and the result satisfied their standards. The apartment had the unreal appearance of a lush movie set with deep lounging chairs of yellow corduroy, blood red carpeting with drapes to match, a cocktail bar and a number of mirrors that enlarged the room.

Keegan was lolling back in one of the lounging chairs, a hypodermic syringe in his hand. He was watching Sheila Latimer, standing before him, in a black, transparent shortie nightdress and gold, frilly pants. There was a sneering grin on his face.

Sheila was shaking and twitching, her eyes watering, her nose running. Keegan had deliberately kept her fix back three hours after it was due, and Sheila was suffering as she had never known such suffering before.

'Go on, baby,' Keegan said. 'Beg for it. Down on your knees. Put your paws together, baby bitch, and beg for it.'

Sheila went down on her knees: her eyes streaming, begging.

Keegan regarded her, then he looked at the syringe.

'I think you can wait. What's the hurry? You keep begging like that, baby. You look cute.'

Sheila moaned and snuffled. 'Please, Chet . . . it's killing me. I'll do anything . . . please . . . please . . .'

'You've done everything,' Keegan sneered. 'Anyway, I'm not in the mood. Knock your head three times on the floor. I want to see you do that. Go on. baby, knock hard.'

As she was abjectively obeying, the telephone bell rang. Keegan cursed under his breath, hesitated, then got to his feet. 'Keep knocking, baby,' he said, 'while I get this.' He put the syringe on the table and answered the telephone.

Silk's voice sounded tense.

'Pack anything you want for a quick trip,' he said. 'The lid's blown off. I'm right now with Coogan. I'll give you half an hour to get here, then I'm on my way. Forrester and the girl have blown. They'll be talking any minute. Move with the feet,' and the line went dead.

Keegan stood motionless. He knew Coogan owned a fast motorboat. Silk would never panic. If there was to be a quick trip, there would be a quick trip. His brain raced. What did he want to take with him? He turned to see Sheila reaching for the syringe. He thudded the flat of his foot against her ribs, sending her sprawling across the room. Then, viciously, he snatched up the syringe and threw it out on to the terrace where it exploded like a tiny bomb. He ran into his bedroom, jerked a suitcase from the top of his closet and threw his best clothes into the case. He unlocked a drawer in his wardrobe and took from it his passport and a thick roll of money which he always kept by him for such an emergency. He stuffed the money and his passport into his pocket, remembering his gun was in the sitting-room. He had taken it from its holster when he and Sheila had returned to the apartment. He slammed the suitcase shut, then went into the sitting-room to collect the gun. He looked around, went to the cocktail bar where he thought he had left it, but couldn't see it. He cursed, then went over to the radiogram.

'Where are you going?' Sheila asked. She was sitting in one of the lounging chairs.

'Drop dead!' Keegan snarled. 'Where the hell's my gun?'

'I have it.'

Keegan stiffened and stared at her. She had got unsteadily to her feet and moved away from him, shaking, his gun, wavering in her hand, pointed in his direction.

Keegan had never faced a gun before. Always it was the other man who had to face the gun. Looking at the tiny hole of the barrel that could spell death, he felt a surge of panic go through him. He stood motionless.

'Give it to me,' he said, his voice a croak.

She snuffled and jerked. Water oozed out of her eyes. She was the most disgusting thing he had seen in spite of her transparent black shortie and her gold, frilly pants.

'I want my fix, Chet.'

'Put that gun down!' Keegan said. 'It could go off, you little fool!'

He tried to remember if he had left the gun at safety. He seldom did. If he had, he could jump her, but he couldn't remember, and hadn't the nerve to take a chance.

'I want my fix, Chet,' she snivelled. 'I've got to have it.'

He looked beyond her at the terrace. The bits of glass from the smashed syringe glittered in the sunshine. He had no other. He cursed himself for smashing the syringe.

'All right, baby,' he said, trying to control his growing panic. 'I'll get it for you. Just take it easy. Put the gun down.'

'I want my fix, Chet,' she repeated.

Maybe, he thought, if he walked without fuss across the lounge and into the lobby, she would imagine he was getting another syringe. If he could reach the lobby, he could slam the living-room door and lock it. His small eyes shifted to the door and saw the key was on the outside. He picked up the suitcase.

'Just hold on baby. I'll get it for you.'

She wiped her streaming nose with the back of her hand. As he began to cross the lounge like a man walking on egg shells, she said, 'Put the case down.'

Keegan stopped abruptly. He put down the suitcase.

'What's the matter with you, baby?' he said, trying to keep the whine out of his voice. 'I'm going to get your fix.'

'You're going away . . . you are leaving me.' The gun waved dangerously at him and he cringed.

'I've got business, baby,' he said, thinking that Silk wouldn't wait for him. 'Don't worry. I'm going to give you a big fix and you can come with me . . . how's that?'

A violent shiver ran through her and the gun exploded with a crashing bang. Splinters of wood flew from the door.

Keegan cowered back.

'Baby!' His voice was shrill. 'Put it down! Take your finger off the trigger!'

She saw his terror. Suddenly she realized she had him at her mercy. The brute who had tormented her for so many months was now actually shaking and terrified. She forgot the need of a fix. She felt only the need to revenge herself on this man who had so degraded her. She steadied herself, trying to keep the gun steady, then she squeezed the trigger. The bullet ploughed a furrow along Keegan's right cheek. He reeled back, horrified to feel blood dripping down his neck and on to his hands. He made a frantic dive for the door as Sheila fired again. The bullet smashed into his body, throwing him forward. Somehow, he got the door open and staggered into the lobby. The gun exploded again. He went down on hands and knees, blood pouring out of his mouth. Moving like a robot, jerking and shaking, Sheila followed him. He was now coughing and retching, trying to get the blood out of his mouth. She moved close to him as his blood began to make a big pool on the carpet.

She bent over him, whispering the words he had so often whispered to her: vile, disgusting words, then as Keegan's arms lost their strength and he began to settle face down in his blood, she put the gun barrel against the back of his head and pulled the trigger.

The two F.B.I. agents, sitting in their car, had seen Keegan and Sheila enter the apartment block. They were two youngish men, solidly built and thoroughly experienced: Walsh, with mouse coloured hair and a square-shaped, tough face and Hammond, with black hair, small features and bat ears. They had reported back on R/T that Keegan had shown up. They had been told to stay where they were. If Keegan left the apartment they were to follow him.

The sound of the first shot reached them through the open window of Keegan's apartment. They looked at each other, then they slid out of the car and started towards the apartment block. Then as the sound of a second shot came, they broke into a run. They raced into the lobby where a fat, elderly janitor was swabbing the floor.

'Keegan?' Walsh snapped. 'What floor?'

The janitor gaped at him and began to fumble at his hearing aid. Hammond checked the list of names on the wall.

'Top floor,' he called and opened the elevator doors.

Again the sound of a gun shot came down the elevator shaft as both men got into the cage. Neither of them said anything as the cage took them swiftly upwards. Both drew their guns. On the 10th floor, Walsh slammed back the grille and they moved out into the lobby.

Walsh rang the front doorbell while Hammond stood aside, covering him. They waited, listening, tense. Then the sound of another gun shot crashed through the panels of the door.

Walsh looked at Hammond and grimaced. Hammond nodded. Walsh stepped back. He rushed the door, driving his shoulder against it. The door shuddered, but held. He drew back and rushed it again. The lock gave and the door burst open. Hammond was there to cover him. They moved cautiously into the inner lobby.

They could hear a woman crying. They looked at Keegan's bullet ridden body. The top of his head had been shot off; then they edged into the ornate living-room.

Sheila was on her knees, sobbing and hammering with her clenched fists on the floor. When she saw them, she cried, 'I'm a junkie . . . help me . . . I'm a junkie . . . please . . . please . . . help me!'

The black Thunderbird pulled up outside Police Headquarters. Nona Jacey jerked back the pistol grip handbrake and got out of the car. She walked up the worn steps and entered the Charge-room.

Sergeant Charlie Tanner, the desk sergeant, sat behind his desk, prodding his teeth with a splinter of wood. He looked at the girl as she came in and his eyes lost their boredom. Nice looking frill, he thought. Probably she has lost her handbag or her dog, or some goddam thing somewhere and expects me to find it for her. Well, okay, when a frill has legs like these, I'll find anything for her.

'Yes, miss?' he said, leaning forward.

'I want to speak to Captain Terrell,' Nona said quietly.

Tanner sat back and stroked his bulbous nose. He looked a little shocked.

'Is that right?' He shook his head sadly. 'Well, miss, if everyone in this city thought they could walk right in here and talk to the Chief, he wouldn't do any work . . . now would he? Right now, miss, the Chief is busy.'

'My name is Nona Jacey, and I want to speak to Captain Terrell.'

'I'm Sergeant Charlie Tanner,' Tanner said, beginning to enjoy himself. 'I've been desk sergeant here for the past ten years and even I can't walk in on the Chief . . .' His voice trailed away. He blinked, leaned forward and asked, his voice rising, 'What did you say your name was?'

'Nona Jacey.'

Tanner gaped at her. The Army, the Police, the F.B.I. and the C.I.A. had been and were still searching for a girl named Nona Jacey.

'Now, look, miss . . . if this is a gag . . .' he began.

'I am Nona Jacey,' Nona said firmly. 'I want to speak to Captain Terrell.'

'Sure . . . sure . . . just stay right where you are.' In a slight panic, Tanner looked around the deserted Charge-room, wishing there was another officer there. He grabbed hold of the telephone receiver.

'Chief . . . Charlie. I have a young lady here . . . claims she is Nona Jacey . . . wants to speak to you.'

Terrell's voice was calm as he said, 'Send her right up, Charlie, and send someone out for coffee.'

'There's no one here but me, sir.'

He heard Terrell sigh.

'Okay, okay, send her up, and I want coffee when someone is there.'

'Yes, sir.' Tanner pointed to a staircase. 'You go up there, miss, and it's the door right in front of you. Okay?'

Nona nodded and walked up the staircase. Tanner watched her climb the stairs, then sat back and wiped his forehead. He was sure he had only to telephone the *Paradise City Herald* and he would be better off by at least three hundred dollars. What was he thinking? He could ask anything and get it. Nona Jacey walking into Police Headquarters was the biggest scoop any newspaper could buy. He put such ignoble thoughts out of his mind and began prodding his teeth again with the splinter of wood.

Terrell was standing in the doorway of his office as Nona reached the head of the stairs. He looked her over, recognized her description and then came forward.

'Miss Jacey?'

'Yes.'

'Come in.'

He stood aside and she walked into the small office. Sergeant Beigler, just back and slightly bug-eyed, was standing by the window. Seeing how white she looked, he hurriedly moved a chair towards her.

'Sit down, miss,' he said.

'This is Sergeant Beigler,' Terrell said, going around his desk and sitting down.

Nona nodded and sat down.

'What's been happening to you, Miss Jacey?' Terrell asked as Beigler took a chair and opened his notebook. 'We've been looking for you.'

Beigler thought this was the understatement of the year considering thousands of men had been combing the district and beyond for her for the past three days.

'I am not important,' Nona said. 'I have been told by Dr. Forrester to come here and to say he wants to talk to Mr. Mervin Warren.'

'Where is Dr. Forrester?' Terrell asked, leaning forward.

'I know where he is,' Nona said, 'but before giving you the address, I have to tell you the situation.'

'Sure . . . go ahead.'

'Dr. Forrester will see no one except Mr. Warren.' Both men caught the tremor in Nona's voice. They looked sharply at her and both could see she was very tense and making a great effort to control herself. 'He has a capsule of—of cyanogen. He carries it in his mouth. If there is any attempt to arrest him, he will kill himself.' Tears began to gather in Nona's eyes. Her voice began to shake. 'Please understand this: he really will do it. He—he just doesn't seem to care . . .' Her face became waxy. She half started out of her chair, then before Beigler could reach her, she folded up on the floor.

'Get Maria!' Terrell snapped as he started around his desk. Beigler ran from the room. Terrell knelt beside the girl. He cursed the smallness of his office. Lifting her, he carried her along the corridor to the reception-room that smelt of stale sweat and disinfectant. He laid her on the old, battered couch.

Policewoman Maria Pinola, a heavily built blonde came in. Beigler stood in the doorway, watching with interest.

Terrell said, 'Take care of her, Maria. Let me know when I can question her.' Then he returned to his office. He asked to be connected with Hamilton of the C.I.A. There was a long delay. While waiting, Terrell said, 'Check there are no press men downstairs, Joe, and tell Charlie to keep his trap shut.'

Beigler nodded and took the stairs two at the time.

Jesse Hamilton came on the line.

'Nona Jacey has just walked in,' Terrell told him. 'She knows where Forrester is. She says Forrester wants to talk to Warren.'

'You're sure she is Jacey?' Hamilton's voice shot up a note.

'I'm sure.'

'Let's have it from the beginning.'

Terrell reported the conversation he had had with Nona, omitting nothing. He concluded: 'She passed out, but I guess she'll be ready to talk by the time you get here.'

'Okay, I'll call Warren,' Hamilton said, 'then I'll be right over. Watch the press, Captain.'

'I'm watching them,' Terrell said and hung up.

Three-quarters of an hour later, Nona was once again sitting in Terrell's office, facing Terrell and Hamilton with Beigler in the background, ready to take notes.

'Dr. Forrester is at 145, Lennox Avenue,' Nona was saying. 'The apartment belongs to a friend of his who is in Europe.' She paused and looked at Terrell. 'Please don't go there. Dr. Forrester will only talk to Mr. Warren. He will kill himself if anyone but Mr. Warren goes to the apartment. He . . . he . . .' She broke off, her face working and she hunted for a handkerchief.

Terrell and Hamilton exchanged glances.

'Take it easy, Miss Jacey,' Hamilton said gently. 'You've had a rough time. Tell me, do you think Dr. Forrester would take his life?'

Nona dabbed her eyes and nodded.

'Yes . . . I know he will . . . I'm sure he will. He—he just doesn't seem to care.' She shivered, then went on, 'It's horrible. He has this capsule in his mouth . . .'

'Did Dr. Forrester mention his formula?' Hamilton asked.

'Yes . . . he says he can decode it, but only on his terms.' Nona clenched her fists in an effort to control herself. 'He told me to tell Mr. Warren that.'

Hamilton leaned forward.

'What are the terms, Miss Jacey?'

'He didn't tell me.'

'Okay.' Hamilton got to his feet. 'You have a lot to tell us. Suppose you come with me? There are details we must know. You'll be more comfortable at an hotel where you can be looked after.'

She shook her head.

'I can't tell you anything until Dr. Forrester has talked to Mr. Warren. I gave Dr. Forrester my word,' and then she began to cry again.

Hamilton looked at Terrell who got up, went to the door and beckoned to Policewoman Pinola who came in and put a protecting arm around Nona's shoulders.

'You come with me, honey,' she said. 'I'll take care of you.'

When they had gone, Hamilton said, 'Get that apartment block surrounded, pronto! Tell your men to keep out of sight. If Forrester shows, they are to tail him, but leave him alone.'

At Terrell's nod, Beigler left the room.

'When will Warren get here?' Terrell asked.

Hamilton looked at his watch.

'Not before ten o'clock.'

'Do you think she was making sense?'

'Yes . . . I guess.' Hamilton rubbed the back of his neck. He looked worried. 'We're dealing with a nut . . . but a hell of a V.I.P. nut.'

The two men stared at each other while they thought, then Terrell said, 'Do you think we should alert Dr. Hertz to stand by?'

Hamilton hesitated, then shook his head.

'We do nothing until Warren gets here.'

The telephone rang. Impatiently, Terrell answered the call. Federal Agent Walsh told him that Chet Keegan had been shot to death and he had a drug-crazed girl in his hair. What the hell should he do with her?

Detectives Andy Shields and Frank Brock shared the day guard outside Thea Forrester's bungalow. They had been on duty now for the past three days and Brock was sick of the sun, sick of sitting on the sand and sick of the assignment.

He was twenty-five, powerfully built with a bull neck, bulging muscles, a deeply tanned boxer's face, and was not only proud of his beef and strength, but delighted with the impact he always made on various girl friends he attracted to him the way a magnet attracts steel filings.

Detective Shields was cast in a different mould. He was lean, tough and ambitious. He had a knife scar along the side of his face and a broken nose, badly set. He was five years older than Brock and four times as experienced. He regarded all criminals as scum and women as the cause of most crime.

The two men were sitting in the shade of a palm tree, staring out to sea where they could see people swimming and enjoying themselves on the beach.

'This is a great life,' Brock said sarcastically, shifting his heavy weight and trying to make himself more comfortable. 'We sit all day long here doing nothing when there is a piece in there longing for a man like me to give her the works . . . it's against nature!'

Shields had been listening to this moan for the past two days. Brock bored him.

'Give it a rest,' he said. 'This is a job.' He got to his feet. 'I'm taking a walk around.'

It was while he was walking in a slow circle around the bungalow that Thea Forrester opened the front door of the bungalow and surveyed the beach.

Brock caught his breath sharply. What a woman! he thought.

Thea was wearing a cotton wrap that just covered her knees. Her sable tinted hair, her emerald green eyes and her smouldering sex made Brock sweat.

Slowly, she turned her head and looked in his direction. Brock got hurriedly to his feet. There was a pause as they regarded each other, then she smiled. Brock looked to right and left. There was no sign of Shields. He walked quickly across the stretch of sand, up the path to where Thea stood, waiting.

'Hello,' she said. Her eyes moved lazily and suggestively over his powerful body. 'Are you one of my bodyguards?'

'That's right.' Brock expanded his chest. 'Some guard . . .' He looked her over with admiration. 'Some body.'

Thea lifted an eyebrow.

'I'm learning fast.' She leaned a rounded hip against the doorway. 'I always thought policemen were rough, tough and horrible.'

Brock grinned.

'They are . . . I'm the exception to the rule.'

'What's your name, Mr. Exception-to-the-rule?'

'Frank Brock . . . my girl friends call me Frankie. '

'Do they? Yes . . . I like Frankie . . . Do you want a drink, Frankie?'

Brock looked over his shoulder. This was risky. He didn't trust Shields.

'Well, I guess, but I can't come in. I'm on duty. Still . . .'

Again her eyes moved over him, sending an urgent wave of desire through him.

'Are you ever off duty, Frankie?'

'Sure . . . but not until six.'

'How about your friend . . . the one with the broken nose? He looks interesting.' Thea adjusted her wrap and Brock caught a glimpse of the swell of one breast.

'You can forget him,' he said. 'He's a square.'

'Is he?' Thea smiled. 'Oh . . . I'll get you a drink . . . beer all right?'

'Beer would be swell.'

She turned and walked down the passage while Brock studied her hip movement. What a woman! he thought. Boy! Could she and me . . . He felt something hard stab into his back and a voice snarl, 'Make a move and I'll blow your goddam spine to bits!'

Brock stood motionless. He remembered that he was supposed to be guarding this woman against a sudden attack from a maniac. Now here was a gun against his spine. Then he discovered something else. He realized he was frightened. He leaned forward, cowering, waiting, terrified of the death that might come to him.

The pressure of the gun suddenly went away and Shields said, 'Just what the hell do you think you are doing?'

Rage and shame made Brock turn swiftly: made his right fist swing towards Shields' scarred face. It was a good punch, delivered with all Brock's massive weight and strength behind it, but Shields had had a lot of good punches thrown at him during his police career. He shifted his head and got his face out of Brock's shooting range. Brock's fist sailed harmlessly over his right shoulder. Shields smacked Brock across his jaw with his gun barrel, sending him reeling backwards.

A glass of beer in her hand, Thea regarded the two men. She felt a hot rush of blood run through her. Men fighting because of her always moved her.

'You boys enjoying yourselves?' she asked.

Brock recovered his balance. An ugly red mark showed on his jaw. Shields backed away, watching Brock. Then seeing Brock wasn't taking it further, he shoved his gun back into its holster.

'Get the hell out of here!' he said to Brock.

Brock glared at him, his eyes full of hate, but Shields was his senior. He hesitated, then walked slowly down the path and across the sand to the shade of the trees.

Thea said, 'The sheep and the goats . . . the boys and the men.'

Shields looked woodenly at her. 'I'm sorry you were disturbed, ma'am,' he said and turned to go.

'You look thirsty, officer. Would you like this beer?'

'No, thank you. I am on duty.'

She regarded him, then she leaned forward and poured the beer into the flower bed by the front door.

Shields started down the path.

'Officer . . .'

He looked around, pausing.

'I have a blown fuse . . . can you fix it for me?'

Shields studied her, aware Brock was watching.

'My job is outside . . . not inside, ma'am,' he said. 'You call an electrician,' then he walked away while Thea watched him. She let him reach the gate, then she took off her wrap and dropped it on the floor. Under the wrap she was wearing the skimpiest possible bikini. Her beautiful body was nut brown from hours of sun bathing. She ran down the path after Shields. Hearing the thud of her naked feet, he turned sharply. She swerved around him and went on running across the sand towards the sea.

Shields looked to right and left. The beach was deserted. He stared after her, then moved into a quick, striding run. He caught up with her as she was about to run into the sea and he grabbed hold of her arm.

'Sorry, ma'am,' he said. 'You must go back. This is too dangerous. My orders . . .'

She wrenched her arm free and then ran into the sea. Shields started after her, then stopped. Already the sea was washing over his shoes. He cursed under his breath as he saw her swimming away from him. He hesitated, then kicked off his shoes, tore off his trousers and shirt as Brock came running up.

'You going for a swim?' Brock sneered.

Shields dumped his gun holster on the sand.

'Shut up, you jerk,' he said savagely. 'This whore could get herself killed.'

Wearing only his underpants, he took a racing dive into the sea and went after Thea while Brock stood watching.

Thea swam well, but she wasn't in Shields' class. She looked around and saw him coming after her at a speed that startled her. She stopped swimming and trod water. She untied the cord of her bikini and let it float away from her. Another swift movement got rid of her bra. Then she threw up her arms and let herself sink. As she came up gasping, Shields reached her. She made a grab at him, but Shields swept her hands away. She was startled by his expertise. He dived under her, came up behind her, caught her under her armpits and held her so tightly she was unable to struggle. This wasn't the way she had planned it. She decided her best move was to fake a faint. She shut her eyes and let herself go limp. Shields towed her back to the beach, then dragged her up on to the beach.

Brock stood gaping down at her while she lay still, her eyes closed, her breasts heaving as she appeared to be fighting for breath.

'Haven't you ever seen a naked whore before?' Shields asked, snatching up his shirt and throwing it over Thea's nakedness. 'For God's sake! Grow up! They are all made the same way. Get my clothes!'

He grabbed hold of Thea, heaved her over his shoulder and started back towards the bungalow.

Brock stood rigid, staring at the long naked back, the solid buttocks and the long legs.

As Shields kept moving, Thea said, 'You are a sonofabitch . . . but you are a man. You can have me any time.'

Shields said nothing.

He carried her into the bungalow and dumped her on the settee.

'You stay here,' he said, not looking at her. 'If there's any more trouble from you, ma'am, I'll take you down to headquarters.'

As he started for the door, she said, 'Wait! What is your name?'

He turned and looked woodenly at her. She was sitting up, her legs crossed, her arms folded across her breasts.

'Detective 3rd Grade Andrew Shields,' he said.

Then he walked out of the bungalow, slamming the front door.

Brock waited until Shields came to where his clothes were lying, then he said with a sneering grin. 'That was quick . . . how did you like it?'

Shields put on his shirt and slid into his trousers. He gave Brock a hard stare, but Brock couldn't leave it alone.

'How was she, Andy? How was she, you mother-raper?'

'Get ready to pound a beat again,' Shields said quietly. 'I'm turning you in.'

He moved around Brock and headed for the police car.

Brock hesitated, then jumped forward, grabbing Shields' arm.

'Now wait a minute . . .' he began.

Shields threw him off.

'Take your goddam hands off me,' he said and continued to the car.

Brock put his hand on his gun, then took his hand away. He watched Shields get into the car and start talking on the telephone to police headquarters.

Kneeling on the settee, leaning forward, her breasts like two ripe pears swinging from her body. Thea stared through the window at this minor drama and smiled complacently.

The five men seated around the table watched Mervin Warren pace the carpet of his luxury sitting-room at the Belvedere Hotel.

Reading from right to left at the table was Chief of Police Terrell, Jesse Hamilton of the Central Intelligence Agency, Roger Williams of the Federal Bureau of Investigation, Dr. Max Hertz of the Harrison Wentworth Sanatorium and Warren's secretary, Alec Horn.

Warren paused in his prowl and said, 'Can we accept this girl's statement?' He was looking at Terrell.

'Yes, I think so,' Terrell said. 'I think it is unlikely she is lying.'

'She says Forrester has a capsule of cyanogen,' Warren said. 'She claims he will kill himself if any attempt is made to capture him.' He turned to Dr. Hertz. 'You have had this man as a patient for twenty-eight months. How is it you never discovered this capsule? He must have had it with him when he was put under your care.'

Dr. Hertz lifted his shoulders.

'It doesn't surprise me,' he said. 'After all, even with the best security in the world, Herman Goering kept his death pill with him until he was ready to kill himself.'

Warren considered this, then he nodded.

'Yes . . . I suppose so. Do you think Dr. Forrester would kill himself under pressure?'

'Of course.' Hertz had no hesitation. 'He could even kill himself if not subjected to pressure. We are dealing with a personality who does not value life. It is even possible that he might kill himself at this very moment . . . just a whim.'

Warren began pacing again. Then after a minute or so, he said, 'All right, doctor. Thank you. Would you stand by, please? We could need you again.'

Understanding this was a dismissal, Hertz got to his feet.

'Do you want me to stay here or may I return to the sanatorium?'

'You can return to the sanatorium, doctor,' Warren said. 'It is late. I don't think anything can happen until tomorrow.'

When Hertz had gone, Warren came back to the table and sat down.

'It is not possible for Forrester to get away?' he asked Williams.

'Not a chance. The whole district and the apartment block are sewn up tight, sir.'

'You are sure of that?'

'Yes, sir.'

Warren brooded for a moment, then said, 'I would be happier if you and Captain Terrell were on the ground, making completely sure. Could I ask you gentlemen to take care of this operation?'

Both Williams and Terrell knew Warren wanted to talk to Hamilton alone. This was now a Top Secret mission, and Hamilton was of the C.I.A.

They left. When they had gone, Warren said, 'Forrester is right at this moment the most important man in this country, Jesse. We must have his invention. He is talking about terms. I don't know what he means by terms, but whatever his terms may be, we'll have to go along with him, so long as we can be sure he will decode the formula. I have this direct from the President himself. We must handle Forrester with velvet gloves. We must have this formula.' He stared down at the polished surface of the table. 'We know we are dealing with a mentally disturbed man, but according to this girl, he can and will, granted his terms, decode the formula. I have been given a free hand. There must be no slip up. Is that understood?'

'Suppose Forrester walks out of this apartment?' Hamilton asked. 'What do we do?'

'He won't. I have a feeling about that.' Warren lit a cigarette. He felt tired. He had had two meetings with the President that morning. He had had a mad rush to catch the plane that had brought him to Paradise City. He felt the load of responsibility weighing him down. 'Do you know if we can reach Forrester by telephone?'

'Sure.' Hamilton flicked open his notebook. 'I have the number right here.'

'Would you get it, please?' Warren stubbed out his scarcely smoked cigarette.

Hamilton told the operator to give him an outside line. When he got it, he dialled the number he had in his book. As soon as the ringing tone sounded, Warren took the receiver from him.

There was some delay, then a click. A man said, 'Yes?'

'Dr. Forrester?' Warren asked, his voice level and steady.

'This is Dr. Forrester.'

'This is Mervin Warren. How are you, Paul?'

A long pause, then Forrester said, 'Oh . . . I suppose . . . yes . . . I'm all right. When do we meet?'

'I'm just back from Washington. The President sends you his regards, Paul,' Warren said. 'He wanted you to know . . .'

'When do we meet?' the flat, cold voice interrupted.

'I can come over right away.'

'Miss Jacey has told you of my conditions?' Forrester said. 'You are to come alone. That is understood?'

'Yes . . . of course.'

'Then I will wait for you,' and Forrester hung up.

Warren pushed back his chair and stood up.

'He wants to see me alone.'

Hamilton looked alarmed.

'He could be violent, sir,' he said, getting to his feet. 'I don't think it would be safe . . .'

'The President considers Forrester to be the most valuable man in the country right now,' Warren said quietly. 'Forrester wants to see me. I must see him . . . let's go.'

A fast ten-minute drive brought them to Lennox Avenue, a quiet residential street on the outskirts of the City. Both ends of the street were blocked off by patrolmen. As Warren's car pulled up, Terrell appeared out of the darkness.

'I'm talking to Forrester,' Warren explained as he got out of the car. 'On no account are you to take any action without my say-so. We have to play the cards as they are dealt. We take no chances of upsetting him.'

'Dr. Forrester is believed violent,' Terrell said uneasily. 'You are taking a risk, sir.'

'So I take a risk. Where is his apartment?'

Terrell pointed.

'That brown stone building. He's on the top floor.'

'You and Hamilton will come with me as far as the floor below his. You will do nothing unless I call for you.'

'That could be too late,' Hamilton said.

'So . . . it will be too late. If I want you, I will call you.'

The three men entered the apartment block. They took the elevator to the seventh floor. Terrell and Hamilton got out. Warren nodded to them and pressed the button to take him to the floor above.

On the eighth landing, he got out. Facing him was a door that stood ajar. A light came from the inner room.

Warren moved forward, paused at the door, then raising his voice, called, 'Dr. Forrester?'

'Yes. Are you alone?' Forrester's shadow, long and thin, fell across the floor.

'I am alone. May I come in?'

'Yes.'

Warren walked into a comfortably furnished living-room. The walls were lined with books. Well worn Persian rugs made rich pools of colour on the charcoal coloured fitted carpet.

Standing at the far end of the room was Paul Forrester, his face partially hidden by the shadows thrown by the standard lamp.

Warren closed the door and then moving casually, took a chair away from where Forrester was standing and sat down.

'Well, Paul . . . it's a long time since we last met,' he said quietly. 'The President sends his regards to you.'

'Thank you.' Forrester seemed to relax slightly. He remained standing. 'This won't take long. You know all about my formula. We need not discuss it. I have decided to let you have it, but on one condition.'

Warren drew in a long, deep breath.

'You will give me the decoded formula on this one condition?'

'Yes.'

Warren stared at the shadowy figure. He wished he could see Forrester's face more clearly. 'And what is this condition?'

'My wife is to be here tomorrow at eleven o'clock, and we are to be left alone together,' Forrester said.

Warren stiffened. This was the last thing he had expected to hear. He managed to control his expression. His brain began to work swiftly.

'Your wife, Paul? I don't know where she is, but I suppose it is possible to find her. Could you give me a little more time? I am sure she could be here about three o'clock. Would that be all right?'

Forrester remained motionless. There was a long, nerve-racking pause, then he said, 'Yes . . . but not later than three.'

'If I manage to arrange this meeting, you will decode the formula?'

'I give you my word. If my wife isn't here by tomorrow afternoon at three o'clock, then you won't get it. Is that understood?"

"Look, Paul, we have worked a long time together. Why do you want to see your wife? After all, she hasn't brought you any happiness. Why do you want to see her again?'

In a cold, flat voice that was so full of bitterness that it sent a chill up Warren's spine, Forrester said, 'I have left a job unfinished. I happen to be a tidy person. Until I have finished the job, my mind won't rest.'

'Wouldn't it be better for you to forget her . . . after all, she is completely worthless. I want to see you back in your old position with all its tremendous opportunities.'

Forrester moved further into the shadows.

'You have my terms. You have until three o'clock,' he said.

He was starting towards a door when Warren said sharply, 'Paul! Just one moment! I want to get this straight. Am I to understand you will decode ZCX if I arrange that your wife comes here?'

'Yes . . . but she comes alone,' Forrester said.

'You don't plan to do her any harm?'

Forrester made a quick savage movement with his hand, slashing it up and down.

'Why should you care what I do with her?' he exclaimed, his voice rising. 'You have said she is worthless. She and my formula are my property. You have until three o'clock tomorrow.' He went into the inner room, closed and locked the door.

Warren sat for some moments, motionless and badly shaken, feeling his face and hands turning damp. Then he got slowly to his feet and left the apartment.

He found Hamilton and Terrell waiting for him on the lower landing.

'Come with me,' he said to Hamilton. To Terrell, he went on, 'Keep your men here, Captain. I want you to take the guards from Mrs. Forrester's bungalow. Forrester can't get away. I don't want the press to find out we have been guarding Mrs. Forrester. Is that understood?'

'I'm working under your orders,' Terrell said. 'Very well, I'll get my two men back to headquarters.' His puzzled look of silent inquiry went unanswered.

The three men went down in the elevator. Seeing Warren's white, set face, neither Terrell nor Hamilton asked how he had found Forrester.

'We'll return to the hotel,' Warren said as he and Hamilton walked quickly to the waiting car.

As the car rushed them back to the Belvedere Hotel, Warren sat huddled up, staring bleakly at his hands. Hamilton, uneasy, looked out of the car's window at the lights, the long promenade, at the people still bathing.

It wasn't until the two men were in Warren's suite at the hotel that Warren said, 'Sit down, Jesse. We have one hell of a decision to make.' He began to pace the big sitting-room, his hands clenched behind his back. 'Forrester tells me he will decode the formula, but only on one condition.' He paused to regard Hamilton, then went on, 'I don't know if I should tell you this condition . . .' He hesitated, then said, 'It should be my responsibility and my decision, but frankly, I don't feel able to cope with it.'

'I can guess what the condition is,' Hamilton said curtly. 'I've seen this coming. We are dealing with a nut who is in a perfect position to blackmail us. He undertakes to give us the decoded formula if we allow him to murder his wife . . . that's it, isn't it?'

Warren flinched.

'How could you have guessed that?' he asked and came to sit by Hamilton's side.

'Oh, it jells. I have studied Forrester's dossier. I have discussed his case with Hertz. The thread that kept his reason together snapped when he caught his Chief Assistant laying his wife. He killed the man. He was prevented from killing his wife. Hertz says that this unfinished job has been poisoning his mind. For the past months he has been brooding over his failure. If we want his formula, we must give him his wife.'

'We can't possibly do that!' Warren said, shocked.

'I've checked on Thea Forrester. She is no better than a whore. No one would give a damn if she dropped dead right now. We should do this deal with Forrester.'

Warren stared at him.

'Now look, Jesse, we are discussing a human life . . . we're not discussing some animal.'

Hamilton shrugged impatiently.

'That is a matter of opinion, sir. To me, Thea Forrester is an insult to any animal. She is a degenerate and no loss to anyone if she died.'

'I can't listen to such talk!' Warren said without much conviction. 'She is a human being . . . we just can't . . .'

'Sir!' The sharp note in Hamilton's voice stopped Warren. 'May I remind you what you said at the start of this operation? You said we must have the formula. You said whatever Forrester's terms were, we would have to go along with him. You said the President had given you a free hand.'

'Yes . . . I know I said that,' Warren returned, 'but this . . .'

'You have been offered a deal,' Hamilton said. 'We get the formula and the woman dies. If we protect her, we lose Forrester and the formula. If we go along with Forrester, this metal of his will give us an enormous lead over Russia's rocket race. The life of a worthless woman just doesn't balance up with the loss of this formula which will give us security for a hell of a long time.'

'There must be some other way to solve this,' Warren said, getting to his feet and beginning to pace the floor. 'Suppose we get the capsule from Forrester . . . neutralize him?'

Hamilton contained his impatience with an effort.

'We can't take the slightest risk, sir. Okay, there are ways to neutralize him if we are prepared to take a risk. We have a gun that shoots a splinter of ice, loaded with enough drug to knock a man out. But it is not instantaneous. There is a time lag of a second or so. Forrester would have time to bite down on the capsule and he would do exactly that . . . so that idea is out. But why bother our heads about his capsule? We can't force him to give us the formula unless we are prepared to give him his wife. That's the situation.'

'But we can't let him murder this woman!' Warren said. 'I can't allow it, Jesse.'

'I wish I could let you out of this, sir,' Hamilton said. 'But I can't. The C.I.A. are used to this kind of set-up. When someone becomes a danger to the State, it is our job to get rid of him. We are trained to put the State first. The individual means nothing to us. Please leave this to me. I'll take care of all the details. But you will have to deal with Forrester. It would be too risky if you dropped out now and I took over. The real problem as I see it is how to get Mrs. Forrester to go to this apartment where Forrester is. She will know from the press and the radio that he is there. She won't go. You will have to persuade Forrester to go to her.'

Warren stared at him.

'Even if I could persuade him to go to her, how could we explain to the press that he got past the cordon?'

'My men are guarding the back of the apartment block. There is a back exit. I'll get him out. I will take the responsibility of letting him escape. This is too important to worry about details like that. We will have to be careful about Terrell. He won't go along with this.'

'From the press angle, how does Forrester find out where his wife is?'

'She's in the telephone book . . . I've checked. As you say, from the press angle, Forrester finds her name in the book, leaves by the back exit, avoiding my men, steals a car which I will have waiting for him, then drives to the bungalow.' Hamilton paused, thought, then went on, 'You and I, sir, will have to be at the bungalow, watching. When he has done what he wants to do, we must go in with the coded formula and get him to decode it before he changes his mind.'

Warren grimaced.

'I don't think I can do this . . .'

'It's your duty to do it,' Hamilton said, his voice hard. 'You must do it.'

'And then? What do we do with Forrester?'

'You will have the decoded formula. I'll take care of Forrester,' Hamilton said. 'Once you have the formula, you will leave. Then

I will tie up the loose ends . . . it's my job.' He sat forward, resting his hands on the table. 'You will telephone Forrester tomorrow morning early and tell him you want to talk to him again.' Tapping on the table with his long, bony finger, he went on to tell Warren what he was to say to Forrester.

CHAPTER SEVEN

CAPTAIN TERRELL arrived at Police Headquarters a little after nine o'clock the following morning. He had had only three hours' sleep and he was feeling his age.

Instead of his usual cheery greeting, he only nodded to Charlie Tanner who was at his desk, and went on up the stairs to his office. Recognizing the symptoms, Tanner sent a patrolman, at a run, for a carton of coffee.

By the time Terrell had settled at his desk and had begun wearily to read the pile of reports that was waiting for him, the patrolman, hot and out of breath, put the carton of coffee within Terrell's reach.

Terrell said gratefully, 'Thank you, Jack,' and poured coffee into a paper cup.

Beigler and Lepski came in. Terrell put two more paper cups on his desk.

'Go ahead . . . help yourselves.' He sipped the coffee while Lepski filled the cups. He sighed, leaned back in his chair and looked at Beigler. 'What's new?'

'The guards are off Mrs. Forrester,' Beigler told him. 'Tom has the important dope.'

'Go ahead, Tom . . . what have you got?'

'Here's the detailed report, Chief,' Lepski said and laid a sheaf of papers on the desk. 'Lindsey and Silk have blown. Lindsey took a fast boat, heading for Havana. Silk also took a fast boat; destination unknown. The boat's owned by Alec Coogan. If and when Coogan returns, I'll pick him up. It's my bet both men are in Mexico by now. I've alerted the Mexican police, but you know what they are. I've talked to the Jacey girl. She says there was a doctor looking after Forrester and she's given me a good description of him. It's all in my report. Keegan's dead. The girl who knocked him off is a junkie and out of her head. If we ever get her straightened out, she could nail Lindsey and Silk. Lindsey is well known at the Belvedere Hotel. He lived in the best suite rented by Herman Radnitz.'

Terrell knew all this wasn't going to get him anywhere. The investigation was out of his hands. When the C.I.A. took over, he became merely a passer-on of reports.

'All right, Tom,' he said. 'You take time off.'

When Lepski had gone, Terrell said wearily, 'There's something cooking, Joe, and I don't like it. Why let this nut remain in this apartment? Why don't they go in and get him? Why take our men off Mrs. Forrester?'

'Yeah,' Beigler said, 'but this isn't our funeral now. Right now, I can hear my telephone ringing. We've got other things to do.' He finished his coffee and stood up. Looking at Terrell's worried face, he grinned. 'Right, Chief?'

'I guess,' Terrell said, and picking up Lepski's report, he began to read it.

While he was reading the report, Warren, at his hotel, asked for an ouside line. When he got it, he called Forrester. There was some delay as every call on this number was screened. Hamilton had made sure that no one but Warren could talk to Forrester. Finally, Warren heard Forrester's voice.

'This is Warren.'

'What is it?' Forrester sounded curt and irritable.

'I must see you again, Paul. May I come around in about an hour?'

'What do you want?'

'I can't talk on the phone. I will come alone. In about an hour?'

'Very well, but don't think you can change my mind. You have my terms.'

'Yes . . . all right, Paul, in about an hour.'

The line went dead and Warren grimaced. Hamilton, looking tired and jaded, got to his feet.

'Well, sir?'

'He sounds unco-operative,' Warren said, 'but at least he will see me.' He went over to the table where the morning's newspapers lay and looked down at the glaring headlines. 'Life would be much simpler without the press, wouldn't it?' He turned and shrugged wearily, 'Where is Nona Jacey?'

'She's with her boy friend on a plane heading for Jamaica,' Hamilton said. 'I packed them off at dawn this morning. I want them out of the way until we get through with what we have to do. They have been told not to talk. One of my men is with them, although they don't know it. When the dust settles, they can come back, but not before.'

'And Mrs. Forrester?'

'I have one of my men watching her. She is doing nothing . . . staying put.'

Here, Hamilton was wrong. Thea Forrester was busy at that moment packing her clothes. She had listened to the radio, read the newspapers, knew now that her mad husband was holed up in some apartment, and she had decided to leave Paradise City.

She was shrewd enough to know that she no longer had any future in the City. When these numbskulls finally decided to capture her husband and put him back in his cell, the subsequent publicity would frighten away all her men friends. She had decided after some hesitation that she would return to New York. She had men friends there. She would miss the beach and the constant Florida sun, but sun and beach didn't spell money, and Thea was money hungry.

But before she could leave Paradise City, she had to have a get-away stake. She had been told by Detective Jacoby that she was no longer under guard. He had assured her she would be safe to come and go as she pleased. She had spent hours trying to make up her mind how she could raise a substantial sum of money. She had finally decided that Wallace Marshall, President of the National Bank, was her best bet. He was a fat old lecher with a battle-axe of a wife and he would be good for $10,000. She wondered if she should ask for more, but decided this sum wouldn't make him squeal too much and it would be enough to get her started again in New York.

Around eleven o'clock, she finished dressing and surveyed herself in the long mirror on her bedroom wall. Even to her critical eyes, she looked pretty good. She left the bungalow, watched by Agent Mark Dodge of the C.I.A., a squat, heavily built man who was sweating gently as he sat on the sand, behind a clump of shrubs. He held a walkie-talkie set in his hand.

He watched her walk to the garage and he grinned to himself. He had already removed the distributor head and was interested to see her reaction when she found the car wouldn't start. He admired her figure, her swaying walk, and he couldn't imagine a girl built like that would walk to the highway which was a quarter of a mile away. He had to wait several minutes before Thea came out of the garage, her eyes blazing with fury, and returned to the bungalow.

There was now a constant tap on her telephone so when she called the local garage, an Agent at the C.I.A. temporary headquarters promptly jammed the line so she only got the busy signal. After trying for some twenty minutes, she dialled a taxi hire service. Again the Agent at headquarters jammed the line. She then dialled the telephone engineers and the line promptly went dead.

She slammed down the receiver, reached for a cigarette, lit it and her emerald green eyes narrowed as she thought.

Car out of order . . . telephone out of order . . . the police guard removed.

She felt suddenly isolated and frightened.

She didn't hesitate for more than a few moments. The nearest bungalow was a quarter of a mile away along a rough sandy road. She decided to walk there and use their telephone. She kicked off her high heeled shoes, went into the bedroom and put on a pair of flat heeled, rubber soled shoes. Then she went to the front door, opened it and looked out at the vast stretch of deserted beach. She started down the path, then paused. Agent Dodge watched her with interest behind his screen of shrubs.

At this moment, her nerve failed. Suppose she walked into her husband? she thought, and she quailed. She knew this was absurd. Hadn't the radio told her that Dr. Forrester was trapped in an apartment on Lennox Avenue which was at least four miles from her bungalow? Hadn't the police decided she was so safe they had removed their guards? Yet, looking at the expanse of lonely sand, knowing she had to walk down a long, lonely road and remembering the terror when the bathroom door had creaked under the horrifying force of his attack, she turned and went quickly back into the bungalow. She slammed and locked the door, then crossed to the cocktail cabinet and poured herself a stiff whisky.

Grinning to himself, Dodge reported back to headquarters. It was while he was reporting back that Warren arrived at 146 Lennox Avenue. Watched by a crowd of sightseers and a number of pressmen and photographers, all held back at a distance by the cordon of police, Warren entered the apartment block.

This time he found the door to Forrester's apartment shut. He rang the doorbell and waited. There was a long silence. He remembered what Dr. Hertz had said that Forrester could take his life on a sudden whim and Warren became anxious. He rang again, then drew in a sharp breath of relief as he heard the lock snap back.

He waited, then pushed open the door.

'Paul? It's all right. I am alone.'

'Come in,' Forrester said.

Warren moved cautiously into the living-room.

Forrester had moved back and was standing in the doorway leading into the bedroom. He looked gaunt and pale: his eyes cold and suspicious.

Warren closed the door, then said quietly, 'I hope you will be co-operative, Paul. We are in trouble. Don't think we aren't going to agree to your terms, but it won't be possible for us to bring your wife to you. You will have to go to her. She knows where you are. We can't drag her here. The press are outside. She is in a rented bungalow . . . alone. It won't be possible for you to go there until it is dark. It can be arranged if you will wait until nine o'clock tonight. I will drive you to the bungalow and leave you. Would that be satisfactory?'

Forrester looked suspiciously at him.

'You are not trying to be clever, are you?' he said. 'I know you are clever, but don't try to be clever with me. I know it is possible for someone to get the capsule from me before I can use it . . . remotely possible. But you still won't have the formula unless you agree to my terms. You understand that? You realize that the Russians might hit on my idea? I don't think they will, but they could. They will most certainly discover it in five or six years. But by then you will have had a very long start. I understand your difficulty. Very well, I will wait. But remember it is you who are wasting time . . . not me.'

'I will be here at eight forty-five tonight,' Warren said. 'I will take you to her. Is there anything you want . . . food . . . anything I can bring you?'

'Nothing,' Forrester said, then he paused, looking stonily at Warren. 'Yes . . . there is something. I want a barbecue knife. I want a special one. The blade measures four inches and it must have brass-headed nails in the handle . . . a replica of the knife my wife once gave me as a present. You can get it from Drew & Stanton on Main Street.'

Warren nodded.

'All right, Paul,' he said, trying to keep his voice steady. 'I'll get it for you.'

Forrester stepped back into the bedroom and closed the door.

Although slightly old-fashioned, The Peninsula Hotel is still considered the best hotel in Hong Kong. Herman Radnitz only accepted the best of anything and naturally he stayed at The Peninsula.

He had just had a curry lunch and was now in the spacious lounge, drinking Chinese tea and looking through a bulky document, satisfied that the Dam project was going well. In another three days, he could leave for Pekin. However, his mind was not at ease. It was now three days since he had heard from Jonathan Lindsey. By now Lindsey should have had Formula ZCX decoded.

Radnitz put down the document and sipped his tea, his bleak, hooded eyes thoughtful. Had something gone wrong? Why hadn't he heard from Lindsey? As if in answer to his query, a Chinese pageboy approached him, carrying a silver plate on which rested a roll of paper.

'Telex, sir,' the boy said.

Radnitz took the rolled-up Telex, frowning at its length. His frown deepened as he read the heading of the message:

H.H.H.; U (Rpt) U.

This was a code that told him: 'For your eyes only. Ultra Urgent.' He saw the sender was Fritz Kurt, his secretary. He got to his feet, his heavy face stormy, and walked to the elevator. He was conveyed swiftly to his third floor suite. He sat down at the desk and spread the Telex out and looked at it. 'For your eyes only' meant he had to decode the message himself. He took from his waistcoat pocket a thin leather bound notebook, picked up a gold pencil, drew papers towards him and set to work.

It took him a good half hour to decode the message and to realize the operation he had so carefully planned had failed. Forrester was in the hands of the C.I.A. Lindsey had disappeared: thought to be heading for Mexico. Keegan was dead. Silk was in Havana.

Radnitz sat motionless. His dream of laying his hands on four million dollars was now in pieces—like a precious Ming vase dropped by some stupid, clumsy, incompetent fool.

All his vicious rage was turned on Jonathan Lindsey. He had long suspected that Lindsey had been sending money into Mexico City. So this incompetent fool now imagined he was going to settle in Mexico, live on the fat of the land and was stupid enough to imagine Radnitz's revenging arm couldn't reach him.

His hooded eyes like grey, frozen water, Radnitz drafted a brief Telex, coded it, then, sitting back, he rang for Service.

Detective 3rd Grade Frank Brock came slowly awake in the Police house dormitory which he shared with three other junior detectives. He looked at his watch. The time was eleven a.m.

He looked around the dormitory which was deserted. This was his day off from duty and he stretched, yawned, ran his fingers through his dark hair, then reached for a cigarette. He lit it and relaxed back in his small, hard bed.

His jaw ached a little and he fingered it tenderly. That sonofabitch Shields had certainly thrown a scare into him. He really had thought Shields was going to get him back on the beat, but it had only been bluff. But while the bluff had lasted, Brock had been scared witless. Well, okay, one of these days he might be in a position to fix Shields. If he ever got him on the hook, he wouldn't let him off . . . that was for sure!

He drew down a lungful of smoke, coughed, then stared up at the ceiling. Twice he had woken in the night and had seen an image of that girl's naked body as she had lain panting on the sand. What a woman! He felt a hot rush of blood through him as he thought of her. If that sonofabitch Shields hadn't arrived when he had, when she was offering him beer . . . who knows? She looked ripe for it. His face and hands became clammy as he remembered the way she had looked at him. He remembered what she had said: 'Are you ever off duty, Frankie?' and that look in her eyes.

Well, damn it! He was off duty! He threw off the sheet and rolled out of bed. He knew the bungalow was no longer being watched. He went to his locker and found he had a little over $100 put aside for just this emergency. Brock believed in spending money on his girl friends. How about going over there, taking her out to lunch and then taking her back to the bungalow? He thought again of the beautiful naked body . . . imagine straddling that!

He crushed out his cigarette and went down the passage to the shower-room. He shaved carefully, took a shower, patted his face and body with after-shave. Returning to the dormitory, he selected his snappiest suit: a powder blue light-weight. He polished his black shoes, then selected a white and red striped tie. As he dressed he was aware that his hands were shaking and his breathing was hard.

As he went down the steps to the car park, he ran into Detective Andy Shields. The two men looked at each other.

'How's the face, Frankie?' Shields asked, his eyes going over Brock's suit.

'Get stuffed,' Brock said and, pushing past, he went over to where his second-hand Cutless Convertible was parked.

It was 12.35 by the time he had reached Thea Forrester's

bungalow. He had left his car just off the main road, under the shade of some palm trees. His car was well known by members of the police and he decided it would be sticking his neck out to park right outside the bungalow.

He had been told the bungalow was no longer guarded but he approached it with caution.

It so happened that Agent Dodge was unpacking a carton of sandwiches as Brock arrived. Dodge liked his food. He had brought with him iced beer in a vacuum flask, beef and gherkin sandwiches and a large slice of apple pie. It was while he was surveying this little feast that Brock reached the front door of the bungalow and Dodge missed his arrival.

His hand shaking with excitement, Brock rang the doorbell. The door jerked open and Thea looked at him.

'Hello,' Brock said. 'Remember me . . . Frankie?'

Thea was glad to see him. At least he was a police officer and could be useful. She gave him her wide, sexy smile.

'Why, sure . . . of course I remember you. What is it?'

Brock regarded her with the steady, probing stare he used with success with all his girl friends.

'Aren't you going to ask me in? I'm off duty. There was a beer offered . . . remember?'

For a brief moment, Thea's smile was less cordial. Surely this young hick isn't on the make? she thought. But maybe he could fix her car.

'Come on in,' she said and retreated back into the untidy living-room. As Brock closed the front door, Dodge took a big bite at the beef sandwich. He looked across at the bungalow, saw nothing unusual, and leaned his fat back against a palm tree, settling down to enjoy himself.

'Sit down,' Thea said. 'I'll get you a beer.'

Brock sat down. He watched her as she walked into the kitchen and his heart began to race. Why bother to take her to lunch? he thought. It would cost me at least thirty bucks. After the beer, I'll give her the treatment. I bet after being on her own for four days, she's panting for it.

Thea came back with a tall glass of beer and put it on the table. She saw sweat on his face and noticed his hand was unsteady as he picked up the glass.

She sat down, thinking this hick has hot pants. I'd better watch him. I'm alone here. I bet he thinks I'm a quick, easy lay.

'You any good with a car, Frankie?' she asked. 'My car's on the blink. I can't start it.'

'You've come to the right guy,' Brock said and grinned. He took a long drink, then wiped his forehead with the back of his hand. 'I can fix any car.'

'I'd be glad if you would look at mine. I've got a date in half an hour. It's in the garage . . . be nice and fix it for me.'

'Why, sure,' Brock said, his eyes moving over her body and at her long, slim legs. 'I be nice to you . . . you be nice to me . . . huh?'

Thea's face hardened.

'Look, sonny,' she said, 'don't get ideas about me. I pick men, not boys. Does your Chief know you are here?'

'You'll find I'm a man, baby,' Brock said. 'I've never disappointed a girl yet. Let's try. Come on, baby . . . you'll love it.' He got to his feet. His smile was fixed. He could feel the hammering of his heart.

'Get out!' Thea said, staring up at him. 'Go on! Beat it!' She jumped to her feet and threw open the door.

Brock caught hold of her and pulled her to him. He had the mistaken idea that she would be like all the other girls he had seduced. Treat them rough, never take no for an answer, kiss them hard and you had them, but it didn't work this time.

Thea leaned hard against him and then slammed her knees into his groin, at the same time she raked his face with her claw-like fingernails.

Brock reeled back, holding himself, feeling blood running down his face.

She screamed at him: 'Get out!'

Brock rode the agony. He saw her through an out of focus film of red. He swung a long, heavy punch at her jaw, felt his fist connect, saw her fly away from him, crashing across the table, sliding over it, her long shapely legs in the air, then crash down on the floor, the table on top of her.

Brock remained motionless, blood dripping down his face, his hands gripping himself, seeing drops of blood pattering down on the carpet.

After a moment or so, the pain in his groin eased a little. He groped for his handkerchief and mopped at the scratches on his face. He looked at what he could see of Thea: her long legs and the curve of her hips. Her head and the rest of her body were hidden under the table. He hesitated, moved towards her, then stopped. He had been crazy to have hit her like that, he thought. Maybe he had broken her jaw. He couldn't just leave her there. He would have to get her to hospital. He thought of

Captain Terrell and flinched. They would nail him for attempted rape and assault.

Slowly, he crossed over to where Thea was lying. He lifted the table off her. Holding his handkerchief to his bleeding face, he peered down at her.

Her head was at an odd angle. He stared, feeling his mouth turn dry. He hadn't broken her jaw . . . he had broken her neck.

Drew & Stanton was the best Camping and Hunting equipment store in Paradise City: a luxury shop patronized only by the wealthy sporting community in the district. Mervin Warren pushed open the heavy glass door and was met by an alert-faced, pretty saleswoman.

'Good morning, sir,' she said, thinking here was a very distinguished looking man. 'Can I help you?'

Warren was feeling unnerved. He had hesitated to ask Hamilton to buy the barbecue knife. He felt this would have been throwing too much responsibility on to Hamilton, although he knew Hamilton would have bought the knife without a qualm.

'I want a barbecue knife,' he said. He cleared his throat, then went on, 'It has to be rather special . . . a four inch blade and brass nails in the handle. Have you anything like that?'

The girl smiled brightly at him.

'It is our special line, sir. We always stock it. Will you come this way?'

At the counter, the girl laid the glittering knife on a strip of black velvet. Warren stared at it, feeling sweat on his face.

'It's a beautiful piece of steel, sir,' the girl prattled on. 'You must be careful how you handle it . . . it is as sharp as a razor.'

Warren touched his temples with his handkerchief.

'I'll take it,' he said, then looked furtively around the crowded store, fearful some newspaper man had spotted him and was witnessing him buying a murder weapon.

Five minutes later, he left the store with a neatly done up package in his hand. His chauffeur-driven Cadillac was waiting and he got in. He glanced at his wrist watch. The time was twenty minutes after one o'clock. The thought of lunch made him feel slightly sick. He told the chauffeur to take him back to the hotel.

Once back in his suite, he poured himself a big shot of whisky, then telephoned down for a chicken sandwich. He didn't want it, but felt he should eat something.

The package from Drew & Stanton lay on his desk.

It was while he was nibbling at the sandwich, staring out at the busy harbour with its yachts and motorboats moving to and fro that the telephone bell rang.

It was Jesse Hamilton who said he was in the lobby and could he come up. The tense note in Hamilton's voice alarmed Warren.

'Yes, of course.'

He dropped the half eaten sandwich into the trash basket. He finished his whisky, then stood by his desk waiting.

Hamilton came quickly into the suite. One look at his drawn pale face told Warren something bad had happened.

'What is it, Jesse?'

'Mrs. Forrester is dead,' Hamilton said. 'She's been murdered.'

Warren stared at him. For a brief moment he felt a surge of relief run through him. His eyes shifted to the package on the desk. Then the full impact of what this could mean hit him. He sat down abruptly.

'What happened?'

'She was killed by Detective Brock,' Hamilton said. 'He was guarding her yesterday. He claims she invited him to the bungalow, teased him and when he got fresh, she kneed him and clawed his face. He lost his temper and hit her so violently he broke her neck.'

Warren stared out of the open window, his mind busy.

'Do the press know?' he asked finally.

Hamilton shook his head.

'My man was watching the bungalow. He called me first, then Terrell. The Homicide squad are there now. The press will get on to it pretty soon.'

'This is a hell of a thing, Jesse. What are we going to do? How will Forrester react?'

'He wanted her dead . . . well, she's dead. This could be a solution, sir.'

'It could be the solution if he were normal, but he isn't. I must see him. Where is her body?'

'Still at the bungalow.'

Warren got to his feet and began to pace the floor, his face set with concentration.

'Tell Terrell to move her to the morgue,' he said, pausing. 'Forrester is certain to want to see her. Get the morgue cordoned off. The press mustn't know about this. There is a chance if he is satisfied she is dead, he will decode the formula . . . and that's all we care about.'

'I'll fix it, then I'll call you. Will you wait here, sir, until I get it set up?'

'I'll wait.'

When Hamilton had gone, Warren lit a cigar and went out on to the terrace. He had to wait eighty long, nerve-racking minutes before Hamilton called.

'It's all set, sir. She's now in the morgue. The press aren't on to it. I'm sending a car for you.'

'Right . . . have a car waiting at the back entrance to Forrester's apartment block,' Warren said. 'I'm going there right away. If I can persuade him, I'll drive him myself to the morgue. When I leave with Forrester, no one is to follow me. Tell Terrell to have enough police to block off any following car. I don't care how they do it, but they are to do it. No one is to know I'm taking Forrester to the morgue.'

'I'll fix it. Give me half an hour. By then I'll have the operation set up and you can go to see Forrester.'

Warren waited ten minutes, then asked for an outside line. He dialled Forrester's number. After the usual long delay, Forrester answered.

'This is Warren. I am coming to see you immediately. It won't be necessary for you to wait until tonight,' and before Forrester could say anything, Warren hung up.

He moved restlessly around his sitting-room, out on to the terrace, and back into the sitting-room while the minutes dragged by. Then, after twenty minutes, he left his suite and went down to the hotel lobby.

The hall porter came from behind his desk.

'There's a car waiting for you, sir,' he said.

Warren nodded. He went out into the hot sunshine. One of Hamilton's Agents got out of the waiting car and opened the rear door. Warren nodded to him. He was carrying the package containing the barbecue knife. He got into the back seat. The Agent slid under the driving wheel and set the car in motion.

'Mr. Hamilton thinks you shouldn't be seen going through the cordon, sir,' he said. 'There's a rug by your side. If you don't mind, would you please get on to the floor and cover yourself with the rug so the press won't spot you? I'll tell you when.'

'All right,' Warren said.

A quarter of a mile from the cordon, the Agent slowed the car. 'Please get on the floor, sir.'

Breathing heavily, Warren squatted on the floor of the car

and pulled the rug over him. The car accelerated. It reached the cordon. Four police officers, alerted, waved it through.

'Okay, sir,' the Agent said and pulled up outside 146, Lennox Avenue.

Warren removed the rug and got out of the car, clutching the package. Hamilton joined him.

'Sorry about that, sir,' he said. 'I thought we shouldn't take any chances. I have a car waiting at the back. I'll come up with you and I'll wait outside the apartment. I'll take you both down to the car and then to the morgue. You will both have to get down on the car's floor. If the press spot you, we won't be able to shake them off.'

'Yes,' Warren said. He was feeling uneasy and his heart was hammering.

The two men walked into the apartment block and got into the elevator.

'Are you telling him about his wife?' Hamilton asked as the elevator creaked upwards.

'I have to . . . I have no alternative. He is certain to want to see her,' Warren said.

'Dr. Hertz is standing by. I have four men on the staircase in case of trouble. I'll be right outside the door.'

The elevator came to a standstill. While Warren walked to the front door, Hamilton moved silently along the passage and leaned against the wall.

Warren rang the front doorbell.

After a delay, he heard Forrester's voice asking who was there.

'It's Warren . . . I'm alone, Paul.'

He heard the lock turn, waited, then pushed open the door. Forrester had retreated back to the bedroom doorway. In the hard sunlight coming through the big sitting-room window, he looked gaunt and pale. There was a tic developing near his mouth that alarmed Warren.

'I have news for you, Paul,' Warren said, remaining near the shut front door.

'Did you bring the knife?' Forrester demanded. His voice was a little shrill and very aggressive.

'Yes, I've brought it.' Warren held up the package. 'You won't need it. I'm sorry, Paul . . . what I have to tell you will be a shock.' He paused, then said slowly and distinctly, 'Your wife is dead.'

'Put the knife on the table,' Forrester said.

Warren didn't move.

'Your wife is dead, Paul,' he repeated.

Forrester flinched, then he stared at Warren, his eyes remote, the tic by his mouth flickering and jumping.

'I warned you not to be clever,' he said. 'Give me the knife!'

Warren moved to the table, put down the package, then moved away.

'I'm not being clever, Paul,' he said quietly. 'This is something I couldn't foresee. Your wife was killed an hour or so ago. I'm here to take you to the morgue where you can see her body.'

Forrester didn't seem to be listening. He picked up the package, stripped off the paper and looked at the glittering knife.

'Paul! Are you listening to what I am telling you?' Warren demanded, raising his voice.

Forrester reluctantly took his eyes from the knife and stared almost sightlessly at Warren.

'Yes . . . I am listening.'

'Your wife was killed by a police officer who imagined she was encouraging him, but she wasn't. There was a struggle, and he broke her neck,' Warren said.

Forrester turned the knife in his hands. The blade glittered in the sunlight.

'I don't believe you. You agreed to my terms . . . now you come up with this stupid lie,' he said.

'I am not lying,' Warren said. 'I am here to take you to see her. This is something that happened out of my control. Will you come with me? You can see her. She is at the morgue.'

Forrester suddenly seemed to shrivel.

'Are you telling me that Thea is dead?' he said. 'That a police officer killed her? You really mean this?'

'I am sorry, Paul . . . yes.'

Forrester threw the knife from him. It clattered against the wall. The tic by his mouth was now jumping madly.

'I understand . . . yes, you aren't a liar,' he said after a long pause. 'Your people killed her, didn't they? I know all about your professional butchers . . . the State against the individual! You don't care about the individual. There is nothing you and your people wouldn't do to get your grimy hands on my formula.' His voice was rising and he looked wild, his eyes burning. 'I should have guessed you would kill her rather than risk a scandal. You fool! Couldn't you know I loved her? I wouldn't have hurt her. I only wanted to frighten her. She would have come back to me. I could have persuaded her. You had to kill her!'

'Paul! Stop this!' Warren said sharply. 'You . . .'

'Don't tell me to stop!' Forrester cried. 'My formula is going to die with me! I have only remained alive because I was sure Thea would come back to me! Now it is finished! One of these days, someone will discover my formula, but it will take time and time is everything. With time, countries like this country, countries like Russia must grow up—must become adult. This country and Russia are now in the delinquent stage of youth. Perhaps in ten years—perhaps in twenty years—they will learn to understand their responsibilities to the innocents they rule over. Then and not before this formula of mine will be a weapon for peace and not for destruction.' He took a quick step back into the bedroom, slammed and locked the door.

Warren rushed into the pasage.

'Quick! Get in there and stop him!' he shouted to Hamilton.

Hamilton's four agents piled into the room and rushed the bedroom door. The door held. They rushed it again and it smashed off its hinges.

They were several seconds too late.

A coded cable was brought to Lu Silk as he was sun-bathing on the terrace of Cuba's most luxurious hotel, the famous *Nacional de Cuba.* He lay in a lounging chair, wearing a pair of blood red shorts, sun glasses and a straw hat tilted over his nose. On the table by his side was a glass of rum and lime juice, the clinking ice frosting the glass. The cable had come sooner than he had expected. He had been hoping to spend at least a week at the hotel, soaking up the sun and relaxing before he began work again. He tore open the envelope and studied the string of letters and numbers, frowning. Then with a muttered curse, he heaved himself out of his chair and walked back to the hotel.

In his air-conditioned bedroom, he decoded the cable. It ran:

Silk. Immediate. Lindsey. Del Prado. Mexico City. Complete operation. $10,000 *credit your name Bank Nacional de Mexico. Radnitz.*

When Radnitz said 'Immediate' he meant immediate and Silk swore again. He called down to the hall porter and asked when the next plane was due to leave for Mexico City.

'15.00 hours,' the hall porter told him.

'Get me a reservation. I have a quick business trip,' Silk said. 'I'm holding this room. I'll be back in a couple of days.'

He dressed hurriedly. He had less than an hour and a half to get to the airport. Dressed, he threw the necessary overnight things into a small suitcase. From a drawer, he took his .38 automatic. He checked the gun, checked the silencer, then slid the gun into his shoulder holster.

The hall porter rang back to tell him his seat on the aircraft was reserved and there was a taxi waiting.

'I'll be right down,' Silk said.

He frowned around the room. He thought of the ten thousand dollars waiting for him in Mexico City. When the job was done, he would come back and relax maybe for another week. He picked up the suitcase, surveyed himself in the mirror, straightened his tie, adjusted the angle of his hat, then left the room.

As he went down in the elevator, he suddenly thought of Chet Keegan. He missed him. Then his scarred face tightened in a sneer of indifference.

He wouldn't need Keegan for this job . . . it was an easy one.

www.ingramcontent.com/pod-product-compliance
Ingram Content Group UK Ltd.
Pitfield, Milton Keynes, MK11 3LW, UK
UKHW022308280225
455674UK00004B/223

9 781471 903601